"I want you so much," Jenny whispered against Maggie's lips. "I want to please you."

The sheets felt cool against her skin as she lifted her body slightly, anxious to welcome Maggie to herself. Maggie's body was silken firmness. Engulfed with desire, Jenny lay back to accept Maggie's lips, soft and gentle, moving lightly against her forehead, her eyes, her cheek. She parted her lips slowly as Maggie's mouth met hers in a long tender kiss.

Muscles tensed beneath her hands — Maggie's body responding to her touch. Maggie's hands flowed along her body like an incoming tide. Her mouth floated downward, leaving pools of pleasure in its wake. Jenny's nipples stiffened as Maggie drew one, then the other, into her mouth. She moaned and threaded her fingers through Maggie's soft curls.

"Your mouth is so warm," Jenny whispered. "I want to melt and disappear inside you." She caught her breath as Maggie's palm embraced her inner thighs. She cradled Maggie's face in her hands and drew her upward. She welcomed Maggie's tongue and sucked it inside. Maggie's kisses were rougher now, hot and intense, they nibbled at her tongue and lips.

Of OVE and GLORY

by
Evelyn Kennedy

THE NAIAD PRESS, INC.
1995

Copyright © 1989 by Evelyn Kennedy

Printed in the United States of America on acid-free paper
First Edition
Second Printing July 1995

Edited by Christine Cassidy
Cover design by Pat Tong and Bonnie Liss
    (Phoenix Graphics)
Typeset by Sandi Stancil

Library of Congress Cataloging-in-Publication Data

Kennedy, Evelyn, 1939 –
    Of love and glory : a novel / by Evelyn Kennedy.
        p.   cm.
    ISBN 0-941483-32-0
    I. Title.
PS3561.E4263038   1989
813'.54—dc19   88-31310
                                                                          CIP

*To the three hundred and fifty thousand women who
volunteered and served in the Armed Forces of the
United States during World War II; but especially to the
fifty-seven thousand Army Nurses, and seventeen
thousand WACs, who served with valor, in combat
situations, in every theater of war.*

About the Author

Evelyn Kennedy brings a varied background to the art of fiction. She spent several years as a cloistered nun, completed a tour of duty as a paramedic with the military, taught on the University and Nursing School level, holds a brown belt in Karate, writes poetry for her own enjoyment, and admits to being an incurable romantic. *Cherished Love, Of Love and Glory, To Love Again* and *Forever* are her best-selling Naiad novels.

CHAPTER 1

At the first sound of the air-raid sirens, Lieutenant Jennifer Kincade stopped dead in her tracks.

She was alone in London. She knew from an information session held for newcomers at the base that German planes always approached from the south — from Calais in France, across the channel, to the coast of England at Moulston and on to the city of London. Air-raid sirens at the Moulston Base sounded the first warning of the enemy approach. The warning was picked up and repeated by every air-raid siren between Moulston and London. The shrill chain continued north of the city until, finally, four minutes after it was first heard in London, even the distant sounds of warning ended. An eerie and expectant silence settled on London like a steel lid on a pot. It weighed people down and held them fast with thoughts of the terror to come.

Lieutenant Kincade was suddenly aware that people were moving hurriedly around her. She watched, motionless, as streams of people made their way toward the nearest air-raid shelters. Two doorways a block away were swallowing long lines of men, women, and an occasional child. All but a few of London's children had been sent to the countryside for the duration. Jennifer mentally selected the first doorway and had just begun to move when she heard the sound of ack-ack guns in the distance. She stopped, listened intently.

The planes are getting closer, she thought. Then, without intention, she spoke out loud. "It sounds just like thunder. Just like a summer storm."

"Well, it's not thunder, Lieutenant, and if you don't get a move on, you'll find that out the hard way."

Jennifer turned and saw a blonde woman walking toward her, feverishly rearranging two leather camera bags whose straps were entangled. The woman's eyes were very deep blue and filled with energy.

"There's a shelter on the next block. It's usually less crowded than others during day raids."

The woman began to run in the direction she had indicated.

Jennifer couldn't move.

"Lieutenant, if you have a desire to get yourself killed, by all means stay where you are. If the bombs don't get you, the shrapnel will." The woman stared at her. "Come on." She put her hand on Jennifer's arm and pulled her off dead stop.

The strength of the woman's hand and the abrupt forward movement forced Jennifer into action. This tendency to hesitate, to freeze and think before she moved, had gotten her reprimanded before.

"If you hesitate like that O'Hara, you could wake up dead," the sergeant had screamed. "Worse, you could get someone else killed. Don't think — *move*. Head for shelter, or hit the dirt."

She was always fine after that first hesitation, those first few seconds of dealing with her fear. But, she thought, as the sergeant had pointed out, there might not be an after that. She had to break herself of the habit.

She liked the strength in this woman's hand — the determination in her eyes. It seemed only natural to follow her.

They walked quickly down four flights of wooden steps and stood at the mouth of the tunnel. The shelter was a medium-sized underground station. About a hundred people had already settled themselves on the concrete floor of the platform. A strong draft of frigid air howled through the open space that connected the south tunnel with the north tunnel. It made a loud whistling sound as it exited one tunnel and entered the other.

"We can sit over there." The blonde pointed to a small space in the crowd about twenty steps from the entrance. The woman plopped herself down on the cement as casually as if she were seating herself on a

3

beach. Jennifer watched as she leaned her back against the wall and visibly relaxed.

"You might as well sit down. We could be here for a while. It all depends on Gerry."

Jennifer held the hem of her skirt with one hand and sat down as carefully as possible. She leaned against the wall and smoothed her skirt as far over her knees as it would go.

"Did you just get off a flight?" Jennifer asked. The other woman wore tan military slacks.

"No. Why?" the blonde said. The corners of her mouth moved into a smile.

"You're wearing slacks. I thought that was frowned upon in the larger cities."

"Mostly by American brass." She stretched her legs full length and crossed them at the ankles. "Fortunately, as an American civilian, I don't have to follow all the military regulations. Besides, the British have already recognized how practical slacks are for women. The Americans will follow suit."

Jennifer looked at the woman more closely. She was tall, five feet seven, Jennifer guessed, and her body had the finely tuned look of an athlete. She was wearing an Army Air Corps uniform, complete with leather flight jacket. There were no insignia of rank.

"I'm Jennifer O'Hara. Excuse me, I mean Jennifer Kincade." She extended her hand. "I'm still not used to my married name." She liked the woman's appearance. "It's nice to meet another American." She gestured to the tunnel entrance. "I appreciate your help out there."

The woman shook Jennifer's hand. "I'm Maggie Conover. I'm a free-lance correspondent."

4

Maggie's smile was warm and infectious. Her thick crop of blonde hair was short and curly. Several stray ringlets fell casually across her forehead. Her eyes, a dark blue framed by long thick lashes, sparked an indefinable emotion that drew Jennifer into them.

The first tremor of bombs exploding caught Jennifer by surprise. She jumped and held her breath for a second.

More explosions followed. They sounded closer. Jennifer realized that she was trembling. Embarrassed, she looked at her hands and then at Maggie. "I don't know why I react like this," she said. "I'm really not a coward."

Maggie's voice was kind and gentle. "I never thought you were," she said. "Cowards don't volunteer for the Army Nurse Corps." She nodded toward the brass caduceus on Jennifer's collar. "And they certainly don't volunteer for England."

Jennifer felt warmth and acceptance in Maggie's words. Where have I met her before, she thought.

"I'm sorry if I was rude with you on the street," Maggie was saying. "I didn't mean to be. It's just that I can't get to a shelter soon enough when a raid starts. The sirens and the ack-ack scare me to death." She smiled. "I won't even mention what the bombing does to me."

Comforted by Maggie's words, Jennifer said, "Somehow I can't picture you afraid."

A shock wave ran through the shelter. For a moment the ground shook, and dust fell from the cement ceiling above their heads. Jennifer looked upward, wanting reassurance that the roof of the station was still intact.

5

She felt a strong hand come over hers. She looked down to see Maggie's fingers close around her own.

"I'm scared too, Jenny." Her voice was almost a whisper, spoken as if in private. "We all are."

"Thank you," Jenny said. She liked the way her name sounded on Maggie's lips. If I were a man, she thought, I'd be attracted to her.

A shrill voice cut across her thoughts. "Is there a doctor or a Sister in the shelter?"

Jenny pulled her eyes away from Maggie and turned toward the voice. "I'm a nurse," she said, and stood up.

"We need you, Sister. A girl is having a baby over here. She's having a rough go."

Jenny moved quickly to the pregnant girl. She couldn't have been more than eighteen. Despite the cold breeze that swept through the tunnel, the girl's hair lay limp with perspiration. Her too-thin body looked frail and vulnerable, her huge chalk-colored belly loomed like a balloon above her. She was lying on a montage of woolen cloth, a haphazard arrangement of donated coats. The girl's dress and slip had been raised and formed a bright blue line just below her breasts. Her legs, slightly less pale than her stomach, were drawn in and up forming two small arches.

She knelt at the girl's side and felt a sharp pain in her right knee. A coat button. She shifted her position and the pain stopped.

"Is this your first child?" She brushed the hair from the girl's forehead.

"Yes." The girl's voice was as thin as her body. Her face contorted in pain, she drew her breath in

6

sharply as her body lurched upward with the force of a strong contraction.

The muffled sound of bombs sent strong vibrations through the shelter. The girl's eyes looked frightened as she focused on Jenny's face. "Please, Sister, I don't want to lose my baby. It wasn't supposed to be born for another week."

Jenny wasn't used to the English word for nurse, but she had no trouble understanding the plea in the girl's face and voice. "Your baby will be fine. Just try to relax. Inhale deeply through your nose and exhale slowly through your mouth." She watched for a moment as the girl followed her instructions. "Good." She squeezed the girl's hand. "Just like that."

A group of women had formed a semi-circle around the mother-to-be, Maggie and herself. "Are any of you relatives or friends?" Jenny scanned the women's faces.

"I've already asked, Sister. She's by herself." A tall, gray-haired woman answered. "We can help though."

"Good." She moved downward and examined her patient. "Has anyone timed the contractions?"

"They're only three minutes apart." The gray-haired woman spoke again.

Jenny looked up. "I'll need a few things — something to cut the cord with, some thread or narrow strips of cloth to tie it, and something clean to wrap the baby in."

"I have scissors and thread in my knitting bag," a woman said.

"I have a clean shawl and a light-weight blanket," an elderly woman volunteered.

"Great. Is there any way we can get some water and something to put the afterbirth in?" Jenny was beginning to believe these women could handle anything.

"There are some old pans and jars by the water spigot at the end of the platform. I'll start filling them. You can use one of them for the afterbirth," a short woman said.

"We'll help," another woman chimed in.

Jenny glanced to her left and saw Maggie kneeling beside her.

"Just tell me what you need and when," Maggie said.

The girl screamed as her body convulsed with a strong contraction.

"Talk to her. Let her squeeze your hand." Jenny looked down without waiting for Maggie's response. What was it her nursing school instructor had said about the ideal delivery room? She smiled to herself. So much for sterile conditions. Reality never did match the textbooks.

"Hold on to me." Maggie's voice was soft and calm. "What's your name?"

The girl's voice was filled with pain. "Doris Evans. Everyone calls me Dorey." Her voice trailed off into a muffled moan.

"Well Dorey, you have nothing to worry about. My friend is an old hand at delivering babies. We're lucky she's here."

Jenny glanced up and saw Maggie's white fingers in the vice of Dorey's grip. Maggie's eyes were focused on the girl's exhausted face. She was mopping the sweat from Dorey's forehead. "You yell all you want. No one will mind a bit. You'll be taking their minds off the Gerries."

As if following Maggie's instructions, Dorey screamed loudly.

"Help us prop you against the wall, Dorey." Jenny kept Dorey's legs separated as Maggie and two other women lifted her into a half-sitting position and leaned her back against the tiled wall. "It should help the pain and make it easier for your baby."

Jenny inserted her thumb and forefinger into the birth canal and spread her fingers as far as they could go. Almost eight centimeters. "You're almost fully dilated," Jenny said. "I need you to push. Take a deep breath and when you exhale push up and out as hard as you can." She waited for Dorey to comply. "That's it, Dorey." She measured again with her fingers. A full ten centimeters. "Good girl, Dorey. I can see the crown of your baby's head. Stop pushing until I tell you."

Jenny watched as the infant's head moved slowly through the birth canal. It felt warm and sticky as Jenny supported it gently with her hands, turning it slowly so the tiny face looked upward. "Good." Jenny's heart beat faster. "The baby's head is clear. I need you to push again. Up and out as you exhale. That's it. I can see the baby's shoulder."

"It hurts," Dorey cried. "I want it to stop."

"You have to help, Dorey. Push again. Up and out." One shoulder cleared and Jenny guided the tiny body upward.

"No more," Dorey cried. "I can't."

Jenny blinked, attempting to clear the perspiration from her eyes. A hand reached out and wiped her face. She looked up long enough to see Maggie kneeling at her side. "You're doing great, Jenny. I'll recommend you to everyone I know."

She relaxed slightly. "Thanks, I appreciate that." She waited for the infant's other shoulder to appear. "You have to push, Dorey. If you don't the pain will be worse."

Dorey groaned as she bore down again.

"That's it. Here comes the other shoulder. Keep pushing. Up and out." She turned the baby gently as its second shoulder slipped onto her palms. The torso, legs and feet followed quickly. The infant lay wet, warm and sticky in her hands. She maneuvered its teeny body and flicked her index finger and thumb against the soles of its feet. No response. She flicked the feet harder. Breathe. Breathe. Let me hear you take that first breath. She slapped her fingers against the soles, and the baby's first cry spilled into the shelter. For a few seconds all conversation stopped. "It's a girl." Jenny held the baby up so Dorey could see her. There was a round of cheers and applause from the crowd.

"What a beautiful mess." Maggie's voice was filled with excitement.

Jenny checked the baby's airway a second time and laid the child on its mother's stomach. She tied several rounds of thread in two places on the cord.

"Be careful," Maggie said. "She's so tiny."

Jenny looked at Maggie, touched by her obvious excitement and delight.

"Why don't you cut the cord?" she said.

Maggie's face brightened. "Is that okay? I've never done it before." Her voice was filled with enthusiasm.

"Trust me. You're qualified," Jenny said, happy she could share this miracle of birth. "Just cut it right here." She held her fingers between the thread ties, close to the infant's navel.

Without hesitation Maggie severed the cord, and Jenny handed the baby to her. "Wipe her off with that clean cloth and wrap her in the blanket."

Jenny glanced at her watch frequently, timing the interval between the birth of the infant and the expulsion of the afterbirth. Eighteen minutes later the placenta was expelled in one piece. Jenny felt the muscles in her neck and shoulders relax with the knowledge that she wouldn't have to deal with hemorrhaging or other complications.

She placed the placenta in an empty pan and cleaned Dorey with water and a soft flannel cloth. She turned again to Maggie. The infant was nestled snugly in her arms. The tiny pink face, smudges of blood still visible, looked peaceful and warm. In the midst of war, she was fast asleep.

"You'd better give her to her mother," Jenny said. She felt touched by the tenderness she saw in Maggie.

They knelt by Dorey's side as Maggie laid the baby in her mother's arms.

"You and your husband have a beautiful daughter," Jenny said.

"Thank you," Dorey said. "Henry would have been so proud." Her large hands explored the baby's tiny hands and feet. "His plane was shot down two months ago. But I know he's watching us now."

Jenny felt the pain of the war pierce her heart. "I'm sure he is." She brushed the hair from Dorey's forehead. "Do you have family in London?"

Dorey continued to look at her daughter. "Henry's aunt lives in Lincolnshire." She ran her fingertips along the baby's small face. "We'll probably move there. She's all the family we have now." She turned her head and smiled at Jenny. "Except for each other, of course."

Jenny felt the warm sting of tears begin to roll down her cheeks. She wiped them away with her hand.

"Don't feel sorry for us, Sister." The lightness of her tone took Jenny by surprise. "We have more than a lot of people. Some of them have lost everyone. I wish Henry had lived to see his daughter, to watch her grow up. But some have nothing left of the people they loved." She smiled shyly. "Nothing but their memories. I have Henry's child *and* my memories. I'm not complaining. Besides, Henry wouldn't like that. He couldn't stand a whiner or a coward."

"That's it, Ducks," the gray-haired woman said. "We'll show the Gerries what we're made of. What are you going to name your baby?"

Dorey smiled at Jenny. "I don't even know your name."

"It's Jennifer. Jennifer Kincade."

Dorey turned to Maggie. "And yours?"

"Margaret Conover."

"I'll name her after the Yanks who brought her into the world. She's Jennifer Margaret Evans."

Maggie's eyes were shiny with delight. "I like that," she said. "It has a nice ring to it. A kind of magic."

The all-clear sounded and people began to make their way out of the shelter.

"We'll take care of her from here, Sister," one of the women said. "Thank you for your help." She glanced at Maggie. "Both of you."

They joined the crowd and climbed the stairs to the street.

"I could use a cup of coffee," Jennifer said, reluctant to leave Maggie.

"So could I," Maggie said. She put her hand on Jenny's arm and guided her through the crowd. "There's a tea room a couple of blocks from here." She smiled warmly. "You and I have to celebrate Jennifer Margaret's birthday. We've brought a new life into this world."

CHAPTER 2

The Cup and Chaucer Tea Room, small and almost empty, had been a bookstore before its conversion. Floor-to-ceiling bookcases lined three walls, filled with leather-bound books donated, the proprietor told them, one and two at a time by regular customers who enjoyed the warm, friendly atmosphere.

Maggie watched Jenny stir milk and honey into her tea. She was aware of the light musk fragrance of Jenny's cologne. Jenny's wealth of chestnut brown hair reached almost to her shoulders and her chocolate-brown eyes looked like velvet. They caught and reflected the images they saw.

"Why did you become a correspondent rather than enlisting in the military?" Jenny asked.

"I wanted to be in the thick of things. If I'd enlisted, I might never have gotten out of the States," Maggie said. She was drawn to Jenny's physical beauty. "I couldn't take that chance. My father was career military. He and his buddies got together at our house once a week to play poker." Maggie warmed as she remembered her childhood. "There's nothing that compares to a group of retired Army sergeants when it comes to telling war stories. I used to sit on the bottom step of the staircase and listen for hours." Jenny seemed interested. Maggie leaned forward. "Sometimes just the two of us would go to a movie or for ice cream. He'd talk to me about combat and bravery, about the comradeship he felt with the men in his platoon. It was exciting to hear him tell those stories. As if I was hearing the secrets of life. The secrets that made life more precious because it could be taken away so quickly."

"It sounds as if you were really close."

"We still are. My father always treated me like the son he never had."

Jenny sighed. "I wish my father was like that. He's never forgiven me for being a girl."

Maggie raised an eyebrow. "Oh?"

"He's a physician in a small town in Connecticut," Jenny said. "He wanted a son to follow him into medicine."

Maggie felt a sadness in Jenny. She leaned toward her attentively.

"I thought he'd be happy that I wanted to be a nurse." She shifted in her chair, as if she were uncomfortable with her words. "He wasn't. Nursing seemed to drive another wedge between us. Nothing overt. Just distance and innuendo. I've been trying to please him all my life." Her eyes filled with unshed tears. She glanced away and took a deep breath. "It's probably the major reason I married David." She bit her lower lip. "It worked, too. Partly. My father was happy about my marriage. At least he was after David signed an agreement to raise our children as Catholics. He even found a Catholic priest to marry us. Not in the sanctuary, of course. In the rectory." She flashed a sad smile. The pain Maggie sensed in her grew deeper. "David is enough like my father to be his son. He's certain he knows best in everything." She pulled her lips into a thin line. "He and my father agree the only true calling for a woman is wife and mother." The sarcasm was strong again in Jenny's voice. "It's nineteen forty-three and they still see women as possessions."

"That's sad," Maggie said. "And aggravating."

Jenny nodded and leaned toward Maggie. "I only knew him two weeks when we were married." She blushed. "It sounds stupid now, but at the time I was caught up in what I thought was the great wartime romance. I had never even dated seriously before. David was charming and romantic. He brought flowers and called at all hours." She showed a faint smile. "He asked me to marry him the day we met. I thought he was exciting."

She stopped and poured more tea. Maggie didn't speak. She felt sure Jenny wanted to say more.

"He looked so handsome in his uniform. A British Naval Officer. My girlfriends were jealous." Her smile disappeared. "When I talked to my mother about him, she pointed out how pleased my father would be if we married."

Maggie felt an immediate dislike for Jenny's parents.

"She knew David would be leaving for England in a couple of weeks. I think she was afraid he'd get away and I'd change my mind." She exhaled loudly. "I wish I had."

Maggie held her silence and listened intently.

"We've written a thousand letters. I tell him we have problems, he writes back that I'm his wife and all I need concern myself with is my husband and my family. He's suggested I resign my commission and move to England. My assignment here is my idea of a compromise, his idea of defiance." She looked directly into Maggie's eyes. "I'll have to work it out some way."

Maggie wanted to tell Jenny not to wait — to get a divorce now — before she had children. She exercised her better judgment. "I hope you find a solution. It would be terrible to live your life in an unhappy situation."

"Yes. It would," Jenny said. She looked at Maggie, smiled, and changed the subject. "How about you? Are you married?"

"I'm busy trying to become the world's best correspondent," Maggie said. "Success is very important to me. I want to leave my mark on the world." She looked for Jenny's reaction. The dark brown eyes were focused on her in rapt attention. Maggie liked the feeling. "I want to contribute

17

something important to the war effort — the best story — the most thought-provoking article." She grinned. "A Pulitzer Prize."

Jenny was smiling at her, her eyes filled with admiration and trust. The feeling lifted Maggie and intensified her attraction to Jenny. She felt as if she were talking to an old friend — a friend she had known all her life, someone she had known before this life.

"I'll bet you do it," Jenny said. Her voice vibrated with enthusiasm. "I want an invitation to the ceremony — and the party."

"You've got it," Maggie said. She felt her nipples grow firm in response to Jenny. She wanted to reach across the table, take Jenny's hand, and tell her all the dreams that set a fire in her heart. Too risky, she thought. Far too soon, far too dangerous. She was leaning so far forward that she lost her balance. Her chair skidded on the hardwood floor and Maggie barely stopped herself from falling. Her hand caught the edge of the table and blocked her forward motion. Damn. Her heartbeat quickened. Breaking my ass probably won't endear me to her.

"Are you all right?" Jennifer looked concerned.

"I'm fine. The leg on this chair is a little wobbly."

"They should fix it. You could have broken something," Jennifer said.

"I'll mention it to the waiter before we leave." She eased back in the chair.

Good save, Conover. She doesn't realize that your attraction for her almost put you on the floor. She relaxed into her feelings for Jenny — warmth, trust, enjoyment, friendship, attraction. They made her feel

18

like a child who had just discovered a best friend — a kindred soul who would share her dreams and adventures. Another self who would be as happy as she was for her successes. She felt a tightness below. A desire to touch Jenny in a sexual way. A need to know the softness of Jenny's lips against her mouth, to take Jenny into her arms and explore the curves of her body. There was a wetness between her thighs. She reached across the table and held Jenny's fingers. The skin was smooth and soft and it felt cool against the heat of her body. She looked at the long delicate fingers, the nails short and free of polish, and tightened her hand around them. They grew warm inside her palm. Desire for Jenny swept through her, but she dared not go further. "We'd make a good team," she said. Her eyes rested on Jenny's, and for a moment there was silence between them. What am I doing, she thought. The woman is married. She smiled and released Jenny's hand. Jenny didn't move or break her gaze.

"We really would," Jenny finally said. "I hope we can see a lot of each other. I could use a friend."

"So could I," Maggie said. She felt the flames of danger kiss her heart.

CHAPTER 3

The dining room at the Savoy Hotel was warm and spacious. White linen tablecloths and a small vase of dried wild flowers on each table lent an air of elegance and order in a world where both were scarce. The room was almost full when Maggie and Christine Ellis were seated at a table on the far side of the dance floor. The orchestra was playing, and a handful of couples were dancing to "It Had To Be You."

At thirty-three, Captain Christine Ellis was a strikingly attractive woman. Tall and sleek, with dark hair and pale blue eyes, she wore very light makeup and a medium shade of red lipstick. Her British Army uniform added a rakish dash of mystery to an already engaging appearance.

Christine had joined the military several months before England declared war on Germany. Her intellectual brilliance had earned her a degree in theoretical mathematics from Oxford, and graduation fifth in her class. She synthesized information rapidly and the British Army was quick to recognize her special gifts. They assigned her to cryptography and cryptoanalysis. Codes are the life blood of any war; mathematics is the heart of any code. Since she had spoken fluent German and French in her travels as a child, she advanced even more rapidly than Intelligence had expected.

Maggie was sure that it was Christine's ability to reach judgments without the distorting effects of emotions, combined with a tremendous capacity for love, which allowed her to accept Maggie's relationship with her younger sister. In a world that condemned them, she and Ann had found loving acceptance from Christine, right to the point of Ann's death.

The waiter took their order, and for a few minutes they watched the dancers in silence.

"Would you like to dance?" Christine asked and winked at Maggie.

"That would certainly take everyone's mind off the war." Maggie bit into a carrot stick. "Don't look now, but here comes the American Army."

A tall young lieutenant was at the table in a matter of seconds. He smiled at Maggie. "Would you like to dance?"

"Thank you, Lieutenant, not tonight." She watched as the young man rejoined his table of three other Army officers. "I wish I knew of a way to let them know before they ask. They always look so disappointed."

"Only until the next woman they ask says yes," Christine said. She glanced at Maggie, and they both laughed.

"Touché," Maggie said. She enjoyed Christine's sense of humor. "I wish we could hang an 'unavailable' sign on our table. I get tired of being interrupted."

"I bet you'd feel different if a few of the female officers asked you to dance," Christine teased. "Besides, you should be used to it by now," Christine said. "You're a very attractive woman. It's not likely they'll stop asking you."

"Maybe," Maggie grinned. "I'll let you know when it happens. Until then, you're lucky you're a captain. At least the enlisted men and lieutenants don't bother you."

"Rank has its privileges. You can always apply for a commission in the British Army. The uniform would look good on you."

"Thanks anyway," Maggie said. "If I'm this attractive without makeup and just a little lipstick, I'd hate to think what a uniform would do." She grinned. "I'll just keep saying no as politely as possible." She bit into another carrot stick.

"I almost forgot. I saw a copy of your article on women in the Royal Air Force," Christine said. "It's very good. One of the best you've written."

Christine's eyes were bright with pride. Maggie warmed under the caring and love she saw in them.

She's so much like Ann, Maggie thought. Same eyes. Same voice.

"Thank you," Maggie replied. "I appreciate your opinion. Even if you are my most lenient critic."

"That's not true. I read your work with a critic's eye." Christine feigned hurt.

"If all my critics read with your prejudices, I'd have a Pulitzer by now," Maggie joked.

"I'm not that easy," Christine protested.

The waiter arrived with their food.

"You couldn't prove it by me," Maggie said, picking up their conversation. She stabbed a Brussels sprout and moved it to the side of her plate. "Not that I'm complaining. I enjoy unconditional love and admiration," she teased.

"You're insufferable," Christine said. "Ann spoiled you rotten."

Memories of Ann were part of Maggie's being. Her face, her laugh, her touch. It all came back too easily.

Maggie's eyes focused again on Christine's face. "I miss her, Chris." She felt tears slide over her lips. The taste of salt and memories was sharp.

"I know you do," Christine said. "I also know that Ann would want you to be happy. She loved you so much, Maggie. She wouldn't want you to be lonely."

"I'm trying, Chris. I really am." She took a deep breath and pushed the memories of Ann deep inside her. "In fact, I met someone I actually felt attracted to. It's the first time since Ann's death that I wanted to ask someone out."

"So?" Christine leaned toward Maggie. "Why didn't you? Ann's been dead for more than a year. It's time you got on with your life."

"The woman is married." She filled Christine in on her meeting with Jenny. "I don't know if she'd be interested if she weren't married."

"I see your problem."

Maggie saw a young Naval officer heading for their table. "We are about to be assaulted by the British Navy. This one may want you. He's a senior Lieutenant."

"I need a sign that says 'I hate to dance. Please don't ask me.' " Christine said. "Observe the finesse and polish I use when I say no."

"Christine Ellis?" the young man said, smiling. "It is you."

"David!" Christine stood and wrapped her arms around the young officer. "God, it's good to see you. What are you doing in London? I thought you were assigned to sea duty."

"I'm on my honeymoon. Right now we're waiting for a table so we can get something to eat. It looks as if we may starve first. There's an hour's wait." He smiled, showing teeth that looked even whiter against his wind-burned skin. His auburn hair and light blue eyes betrayed a Celtic ancestry.

"If you don't mind that we've already started, you're welcome to share our table. You can fill me in on what you've been doing since the war started."

"Sounds great," David said. He turned to Maggie. "That is, if your friend doesn't mind."

"I'm sorry. I'm forgetting my manners." Christine looked at Maggie. "Maggie Conover, this is David Kincade. David is a ghost from my past. We were at Oxford together. He's a statistician when he's not fighting a war. Do you mind if he and his wife join us?"

"Not at all," Maggie said. "I think I've met your wife. I watched her deliver a baby." She was amazed at this coincidence, excited and apprehensive at the thought of seeing Jenny again.

"So, you're the tomboy journalist Jenny has been raving about." He extended a hand. "Jenny will be so pleased to see you again. I've heard about you and her playing doctor in the Underground." He smiled. "You made a real impression on her with your heroics. Let me get her."

As soon as he left she said, "He talks like a jerk."

"He can be, but I think you're the one who's prejudiced now. You're letting your feelings for his wife color your feelings for him," Christine said. "He's not perfect, but he's not a monster. He can be a very loyal friend."

Maggie was annoyed by Christine's defense of David. She didn't want to like him, and she didn't want to know how wonderful he could be. If only her feelings for Jenny were not completely futile. So far, Christine hadn't given her any hope.

"You know me well enough to know that I'm not about to get involved with someone who's already committed," Maggie said. "Besides, I don't know if Jennifer Kincade could be attracted to a woman. She certainly doesn't need any more complications in her life. She's already wrestling with the church's view of divorce. That battle would not compare to the one she'd go through if she got involved with a woman." Maggie swallowed some cold coffee. "I'm attracted to her, but that doesn't mean we can't be friends." She laughed. "It's ironic that the only woman I've been interested in since Ann's death turns out to be

25

married to a friend of yours. This hasn't been my year. I'll be glad to see nineteen forty-four."

David returned to the table with Jenny. He introduced her to Christine and as he gave the waiter their order, Maggie extended a hand to Jenny. "It's good to see you again. I hoped we'd run into each other at the hotel," Maggie said.

What is it about her, she thought. She had never reacted this way to anyone before, not even Ann. She was unable to look at anyone else. Jenny's uniform fit her body perfectly. It clung to all the soft curves underneath and swelled gracefully over her large breasts. She imagined Jenny's nipples erect against the cloth that covered them. Maggie felt her heart rate increase just before she felt the butterflies in her stomach.

"I'm surprised anyone got David to settle down," Christine was saying. "He had a timetable for his entire life when we were in school." She looked from Jenny to David. "If I remember correctly, marriage and family aren't due for four or five more years."

"The war changed that," David said. "It's given a sense of urgency to everything." He put his large hand over Jenny's, hiding hers completely. "We'll start our family as soon as the war is over."

Maggie watched Jenny's face. Her eyes flashed anger, but it was gone as quickly.

Maggie said, "You'll have your hands full with a baby and a nursing career. I don't see how anyone could manage both."

"We don't plan for Jenny to continue in nursing," David said. "Once we start a family, she'll be a full-time wife and mother."

26

Jenny blushed and moved her hand away from David's.

"Have I embarrassed you?" David asked. His blue eyes sparkled with boyish mischief. He reached for Jenny's hand and surrounded it again. "I'm sorry. I forget how shy you are. Besides, Christine is married."

Maggie saw the discomfort on Jenny's face and for a moment she wanted to hit David. How could anyone be so insensitive, she thought. He obviously hadn't discussed this with her.

"Jenny still has some acclimating to do. She's not used to British ways," David said.

"If Jenny is uncomfortable with the subject, why don't you choose another," Maggie said.

David glared at Maggie for a moment. He's deciding how to take my remark, she thought. The hell with him. I don't care if he is offended. He treats her like a retarded child.

David turned toward Maggie. "How long have you been in England?" His tone was casual.

"Since May of nineteen thirty-nine," Maggie said.

The waiter arrived with their food.

"It must have been difficult for you to get work as a journalist. I wouldn't think too many papers were looking for a female correspondent," David said.

"You're right about that. I worked for a small British weekly at first. I did everything from making coffee to typing, to writing fillers." Maggie could feel Jenny's eyes on her. "When war was declared, I used my knowledge of England and my contacts here to get in as a free-lance writer for several papers in the States. I've been able to broaden my base from there.

27

They don't pay me very much, but at least I get a by-line now."

David's features hardened. "You certainly can't expect to be paid as much as a real correspondent," David said. He broke off a piece of bread and crushed it between his fingers.

"Why not?" Maggie could feel the anger rising in her throat.

"Gals don't need that much money. You don't have to support a family. When the war's over, you'll get married and settle down. It just wouldn't make sense to pay a girl as much."

"And what if I don't get married? My family can't support me!" Maggie fought to control her anger.

"You're an attractive girl. You'll get a husband," David said. "You'll have to change some of your attitudes to keep him, but you'll catch a man."

Maggie was furious. She fought to maintain her silence.

"Maggie, please, this isn't the time or place for this," Christine said. She put her hand on Maggie's arm.

"What did I say?" David asked. He looked from Christine to Jenny. "I tried to pay her a compliment."

"David, that sounds terrible. You owe Maggie an apology," Jenny said.

"I intended to pay her a compliment. If I hurt anyone's feelings, I apologize." He looked at Maggie. "Will you accept my apology, Maggie? I don't want to end the evening on a sour note."

Maggie felt Christine's fingers digging into her arm. She looked at Jenny and recognized her silent plea for peace. She took a deep breath and swallowed her anger. "I accept."

"Fair enough," David said.

She turned toward Jenny. "Have you gotten to see any of London?"

"I explored a little on my own while David was in classes at the admiralty," Jenny said. "I got lost. There are an awful lot of missing street signs out there."

"I get lost and I was raised here," David said. His eyebrows rose in emphasis. "The bombings have changed everything. Street signs, landmarks . . ." He took a swallow from his cup. "Maybe you could show her around, Christine? Sort of get her used to the neighborhood around Saint Elizabeth's."

"I'd like to, David, but my hours are so erratic I never know when I'll have free time," Christine said.

"How about you, Maggie?" Jenny asked. "Could you spare the time?"

"I'd be happy to show you around. Besides, you can do me a favor in return. I've been trying to get an interview with the Chief Matron at Saint Elizabeth's. Maybe you can arrange it for me in the next couple of months."

"That shouldn't be a problem," Jenny said. "We've met several times, and we get along well."

"Good," Maggie said. "When are you free?"

"I'll be working regular hours. Seven to three, Monday through Friday. It's one of the advantages of teaching," Jenny said. "Could you meet me in front of the hospital around three-thirty on Tuesday?"

Maggie kept her voice calm and casual. "I'll be there." Inside she was elated.

CHAPTER 4

Jenny rinsed her toothbrush and stared into the bathroom mirror. The sound of the shower had a hypnotic effect on her. She could hear David singing in the background. A thin wet layer of steam obscured her reflection in a milky haze. The glass felt cool on her hand as she cleared a lopsided circle out of the mist. How can I look the same and feel so different, she thought. I should be happy that David wants a family. I wanted a family. I can't have changed that much.

She pushed for clarity. Thoughts and feelings collided in a confusing mass. Steam was forming again on the mirror. It moved inward from the edges of the circle, veiling her image in fuzzy softness. She could still recognize her features, but the details were lost to her. A shape, the outline of her mouth, the barest suggestion of her eyes. The mist covered them completely. A fog that hid her from herself.

The cadence of the shower changed. Jenny moved into the bedroom and propped herself against her pillow. Maybe if I talked to him again he'd understand, she thought. Maybe I'll understand. Her eye caught David's reflection in the dresser mirror. She watched as he wrapped a towel around his narrow hips.

She registered his broad shoulders, his muscular back, his well-developed arms. Any woman would think him handsome. He is handsome. Why don't I feel excited with him? He's my husband. I thought marriage would make it different, would make me feel sexually attracted to him.

Air banged its way through old pipes. David had turned the water off in the sink. He would be there in a minute and she would talk to him again, make him understand how important nursing was for her. If he understood one, he'd understand the other.

David walked into the bedroom. "What did you think of Christine?" He plopped himself on the bed and used his pillow to brace his neck.

"She seems nice. I hope I get to spend some time with her later." She could feel the fluttering in her stomach. Go ahead and talk to him, she thought.

"I do too," David said, "I'm not really crazy about you spending time with Maggie. I'm sorry you asked her to show you around."

"Why? Because you had a disagreement with her?" Jenny felt her anger flare.

"Because she's obnoxious. Our family life is none of her business. I resent her comments about our personal life. I didn't ask for her opinion."

"I think she's gutsy. She doesn't have any trouble saying what she feels. Besides, your remarks to her weren't exactly hostility-free."

"What I said was true." David's face was slightly flushed. "No man would want a girl with her ideas. She sounds like a nut, or a man-hater. I don't know why Christine bothers with her."

"Maybe she enjoys the company of a woman who can think for herself. I admire her." Jenny knew she was pushing David's beliefs to the wall. Right now she didn't care.

"That surprises me." David's face was scarlet. "Since when do you admire sexual deviates? That's what she is, you know. I'd bet on that."

"How unfair to say that." Jenny resented his attack on Maggie. "You don't even know her."

"I know enough to recognize there's something wrong with her. The girl doesn't like men." David's tone was strident.

"Maybe it's just you she dislikes. You certainly gave her reason enough." Jenny was surprised at her own words. Her anger at him had reached the point where truth was spoken without a thought for the consequences. "You talk to women as if they're all the same. Any woman would resent your attitude."

For a moment David looked stunned, as if her words had caught him like a hammer. He stared at her in silence for several seconds. "I didn't realize you felt like that. Why didn't you bring it up before now?"

"I tried to." Jenny softened her voice. "You never listened. I wrote you about it many times." She felt the frustration of past attempts to communicate with David. "You never mentioned the subject. It was as if I'd said nothing."

David shifted his position and realigned himself against his pillow. "I'm listening now. What do you want to tell me?"

Jenny looked at his angry face. Dear God, she thought, is communication always this difficult? Is it my fault for not insisting that he deal with the problems?

"I'm waiting," David said. His tone was frigid.

"Honey, I'm not criticizing you. I want our marriage to work." Jenny moved forward and turned to face him. "If I didn't care I wouldn't be trying to work it out. I know I'm at fault for not insisting earlier that we talk. I can't change that, but maybe together we can change the present."

"Go on," David said. His tone was cold, his body tense.

"I want you to hear how important my career is to me. How important it is for me to contribute whatever I can to the war effort." She let go of her defenses and spoke from her heart. "I can't go into battle, I can't fly a bomber over Germany, or shoot down Japanese planes." She took his hand. "But I can do something about the wounded. I can ease their pain, and I can help save lives." She looked deep into

33

his eyes. "Please don't ask me to give that up. I was an Army nurse when we met. It never occurred to me that you would want me to resign. I wouldn't have married you if I had known that."

"Are you saying that you'd leave me for your nursing career?" David said. His face was a mixture of anger and hurt.

"No, of course not. You're my husband. I've made a commitment to you." She brushed several strands of auburn hair from his forehead. "But I made a commitment to nursing and to the war effort before I met you. I want to honor those commitments too. If I didn't, I'd lose respect for myself."

"I don't understand you," David said. "No one expects a girl to choose the military or a career above her husband's wishes." His eyes showed the barest signs of relenting. "But if it means that much to you, keep your damn commitment. But only until you get pregnant."

"Fair enough," she said, encouraged by his words.

"What was the other thing you wanted to talk about?" David said. "We might as well get everything solved at once."

Jenny took a deep breath and rubbed her palm across David's hand. She looked deeply into his pale blue eyes. "It's when we make love." She felt the muscles in his hand tighten. "Either I feel nothing, or the little excitement I do feel doesn't go anywhere."

David's face was scarlet. He pulled his hand away and glared at her. "What the hell do you expect to feel? We've only been married a short time. We've spent most of that time away from each other. I'm not a miracle worker."

"I'm not blaming you, honey. It's not your fault. I just thought if we could change a few things . . . take more time . . . that it would be better for both of us."

"You're damned right it's not my fault. I've made love to you straight from the book. I didn't leave anything out."

Jenny felt as if he had punched her in the stomach. Why does this have to be so hard, she thought. "I'm not complaining." She took his hand. "Please hear me. I only want to make things better for us."

"Things are fine for me. I don't need a change." He pulled his hand away again. "You want to make things better for yourself."

"That isn't true," Jenny said. She felt deeply hurt by David's words.

"What kind of girl are you?" His face and voice were filled with disgust. "Wives don't give sex instructions to their husbands. They do what he asks. Have I asked for anything unnatural?"

"No, of course not." Jenny felt thoroughly defeated. "You've misunderstood what I was saying."

"I don't think so," David said. "But if you insist, we'll slow down a little — beginning now." He got up and began to dress.

"Where are you going?" Jenny asked.

"For a walk."

"Don't go, David. I really want to work this out."

"Then act like it. Stop criticizing me. There are things a man doesn't want to hear from his wife." He stopped buttoning his shirt and sat on the bed. "I respect you. I want you to have my children. I don't think of you like some slut who'd do anything for her appetites."

David put his arms around her. "You're just confused." He kissed her on the forehead and looked into her eyes. "Stop worrying about our love life. I'm perfectly satisfied. I don't know where you get the idea that I want you to be different in bed. You're just fine the way you are." He held her close.

The tightness in her throat had lessened. She felt the warmth of tears roll slowly down her face. I can't make him understand, she thought. He doesn't want to hear me.

CHAPTER 5

Maggie was glad to see Jenny waiting when she arrived at Saint Elizabeth's. She had been looking forward to their meeting all day. Now in the cool October afternoon, she took delight in Jenny's rosy complexion and warm smile.

"I hope you like to walk," Maggie said. "I plan to show you a lot of the city."

"I love to walk," Jenny said.

"Good. We can start that way." Maggie pointed toward a side street ahead and to the right.

"Lead on MacDuff," Jenny said. She fell into step with Maggie.

"I haven't met any nurses before who quote Shakespeare," Maggie joked. She glanced at Jenny.

"You've obviously been meeting the wrong nurses," Jenny said. They turned the corner onto the side street.

The buildings were mainly one-, two-, and four-family houses. Occasionally a six-family apartment building rose above the roofs of the houses. They looked like tall strangers who had lost their way. Three barrage balloons floated above the block, their long steel cables tethered to large metal hooks pounded into the ground to hold the huge balloons in place. They looked like inflatable toys for the children of giants. They were, in fact, instruments of defense.

"When I first saw those things," Jenny said as she pointed at one of the balloons, "I couldn't figure out what they were for. It doesn't look as if they worked too well here."

Maggie looked at the long street in front of her. Two houses down on the left, a large vacant space ended in a wide, rubble-filled crater. A makeshift wooden barricade stood in front of the lot with a hand-painted sign nailed to one of the boards that read, DANGER — KEEP OUT. The first barrage balloon was anchored at the lip of the crater. Its wide, pudgy blimp shape floated like a ghost above the destruction.

"Unfortunately London was blitzed before they could get all the balloons up," Maggie said. They walked toward the crater. The smell of rubble and dampness assaulted her nostrils. "The smell always reminds me of an old, neglected house. One that sunlight hasn't entered in years."

"That's exactly what it smells like," Jenny said.

Maggie glanced upward. "The balloons do keep the Gerries from flying lower than nine thousand feet. They make strafing impossible and foul up the pilot's view of the target." They reached the edge of the crater. "As you can see," Maggie said, "the balloons don't stop the bombs."

Jenny rested a hand on the top plank of the barricade. "I wonder what happened to the people who lived here. Maybe they made it to a shelter."

"Chances are they were right there when the bomb struck," Maggie said. She felt a hint of the anger and frustration the bombings had fomented in her. "People get tired of going to air-raid shelters every night. They become fatalists." She took a deep breath. "Short-lived fatalists."

They began to walk again, past another crater, another pile of rubble, a house with only half a roof. Jenny's shoe caught on a broken place in the pavement. She stumbled forward. Maggie moved quickly catching her in both arms and drawing her body against her own. She could feel the swell of Jenny's breasts, soft against her own. Jenny's breath felt warm as it brushed against her mouth. They were closer than they had been before, locked in this accidental embrace. Maggie's arms pulled Jenny closer. She saw herself lean forward and kiss Jenny's full lips. Her mouth would be soft and warm, she thought. Her muscles tightened below. I really want her, she thought. I'd like to make love to her right now.

Suddenly, she was aware that Jenny was stepping back. She opened her arms reluctantly.

"Thank you. That could have been a nasty fall."

Maggie wanted to pull her back inside her arms and cover her mouth with kisses. She inhaled deeply and nodded. They started walking again.

"Why don't they rebuild?" Jenny asked.

"First off, they're not allowed to. All raw materials go to the war effort. Secondly, most of their young craftsmen are in the military. And finally, who's to say the same place won't get bombed again?"

Jenny was looking at the remaining wall and staircase of what used to be a house. "People back home don't know how lucky they are. How blessed America is not to have suffered this."

Maggie felt a growing appreciation for Jenny's sensitivity. She watched her closely as she spoke. "The thought of Hartford, or New York, or any American city, destroyed like this, scares me to death."

"I know what you mean," Maggie said. "I feel the same way. In fact just thinking about America makes me homesick."

"Me too. I miss the sounds of waking up at home, my mother moving around the kitchen, calling to my father telling him to hurry or he'll be late for his rounds. The smell of fresh coffee and bacon frying." She smiled at Maggie. "The taste of that bacon, all crisp and hot." She smiled. "Other people may be fighting for Mom's apple pie, but it's hot crisp bacon and fresh scrambled eggs I'd kill for."

Maggie grinned. She felt like a child about to show a treasured possession to a friend who would love it as much as she did. "I'm about to make you a very happy woman," Maggie said. "I can't promise bacon and eggs, but I know the location of the only Italian restaurant in London. If you'd like, we'll go there for dinner tonight."

"I've only eaten spaghetti once. As far as I know there aren't any Italian restaurants in Connecticut. I got to try it at a classmate's house when her grandparents were visiting from Italy." She smiled. "I liked it. An Italian restaurant sounds like an adventure. I'd love to go."

"Great. We'll go after our tour."

* * * * *

They walked through the neighborhood, stopping at two small green grocers — one that always managed to have fresh eggs, the other which rarely ran out of sugar. Maggie pointed out a neighborhood pub called Maxwell's. The owner had had the foresight before war was declared to locate his business in a large cave-like cellar that acted as a natural air-raid shelter. Unlike most pubs and restaurants that closed by eight-thirty every evening, Maxwell's served food from eight in the morning until midnight, every day of the week.

It was a little after six when Maggie and Jenny ordered dinner at Mamma Mia's.

"This is swell," Jenny said. She looked around the small restaurant. "Red and white checked tablecloths, Chianti bottles complete with candle on every table." She inhaled deeply. "It even smells wonderful."

41

"You must have been Italian in a previous life," Maggie said.

Jenny looked thoughtful. "You've alluded to reincarnation before. You don't really believe in it, do you?"

"As a matter of fact I do."

"I'm surprised. You seem too analytical to hold such a doubtful theory."

"It seems logical to me," Maggie said. She leaned forward. "Haven't you ever met someone for the first time and felt like you've known them forever?"

"Just once. I felt like that with you."

Jenny's words excited Maggie. "I felt the same way." She watched Jenny's eyes while the waiter served their food. They were bright and alert, filled with passion, stimulating Maggie's imagination. "I feel like we've known each other forever."

"David wouldn't like that. He's not crazy about our relationship." Jenny tasted her spaghetti. "This is fabulous." She sipped her wine.

"He doesn't like me, does he?" Maggie asked. She watched Jenny's face for her reaction. There was a flirtatious look in her eyes, a look that bordered on seduction. Its possibilities made Maggie warm with desire.

"No, he doesn't." Jenny put her fork down and looked at Maggie intently. "He thinks you're obnoxious."

"Probably at times I am. I can be quite emphatic about my beliefs."

"I think he's afraid I'll pick up some of your attitudes." She smiled. "He doesn't feel you respect men."

"And what do you think?" She fastened her eyes on Jenny's, deliberately leaving the question open-ended. She could feel Jenny's interest in her.

"I like your attitude," Jenny said. "It's much different from what I grew up with, but it makes sense to me."

"Did you tell David that?"

"Yes. He wasn't too pleased about it." She looked at her wine glass, then at Maggie. "He didn't want me to see you today."

Jenny looked directly into Maggie's eyes. Maggie could feel the energy that passed between them. It increased her desire to feel Jenny close to her.

"Why did you come?" Maggie asked. She already knew the answer, but she wanted to hear how Jenny saw it.

"I don't intend to let David choose my friends. I like you. Very much. I don't want to lose the chance at a really good friendship." She flashed a mischievous smile. "Besides, it might do me some good if I did adopt your attitudes. It certainly couldn't hurt."

"You're wrong about that, Jenny. It might hurt your relationship with your husband. David doesn't impress me as the type who would gladly accept a difference of opinion from his wife." Maggie was looking for information.

"He's not," Jenny replied. Her face became serious. "He thinks a wife is an extension of her husband."

"Are you sure you want to risk his anger?" She knew that a positive response would mean Jenny cared enough about their relationship to take serious risks rather than let it go.

"I'm sure," Jenny said. "I need a friend." Her eyes were more than friendly.

Maggie wanted to reach out and take Jenny's hand. She's beautiful, she thought. She watched the red fullness of Jenny's lips.

"You're special to me, Maggie. I feel completely at home with you."

Maggie's eyes riveted Jenny's. Suddenly she was aware of Jenny's hand on hers. It was warm and soft and sent waves of excitement through her. She wanted to embrace Jenny, to feel the full length of her body against her own, to enfold her in tenderness.

"I really want to know you better," Jenny said. Her eyes moved down Maggie's body.

Maggie was delighted by Jenny's words. "I'd like that." She turned her hand to Jenny's. She felt her tremble in response. "I'd like that very much."

CHAPTER 6

Three weeks later, while David was away at sea, Jenny went to Maggie's cottage for the weekend. After numerous dinners and conversations, they had grown friendly and relaxed in each other's company. Both were looking forward to the weekend together.

Maggie parked the car next to the weathered frame cottage.

"It's no mansion, but the view is spectacular," Maggie commented as they walked to the cottage door. "I'll get a fire started. It shouldn't take long to knock the chill off." She pointed to her right. "The kitchen's in there."

Jenny stored the groceries while Maggie worked on the fireplace. The kitchen was small, with a minimum of cabinet space, a refrigerator that looked as if it had been used in football practice, and a square oak table covered with a yellow and white checkered oil cloth. The window over the double sink looked out on a sandy beach and restless ocean. The view was broken by two six-foot-high barbed wire fences, one about seventy yards from the cottage, the other about three feet from the first. They ran in either direction, as far as she could see. Their march was disrupted every ten or twelve feet by a narrow opening. Like the barrage balloons in the cities, the double fence was a defensive device. It was intended to discourage, or at least slow down, any enemy attempt to land in England.

"The fire smells great," Jenny said as she walked into the main room. It was furnished with early eclectic. Combinations of old and new, light and dark, reminded her of Maggie. It had her comfortable look. Two faded blue chairs and an equally faded blue sofa were grouped near the stone fireplace. There was a hand-carved double 8x10 picture frame in the corner of the long stone mantel. Maggie, in flight jacket and white scarf, smiled from the right side of the frame. The picture in the left side of the frame had been removed, leaving gray cardboard behind. An identical frame stood at the opposite end of the mantel. It held a photograph of Maggie and Christine in one side and a blank cardboard space in the other. Jenny wondered why the pictures had been removed.

"Very pretty," Jenny said. She watched Maggie replace the large fire screen. She admired Maggie's athletic build — solid and healthy, as if she could endure whatever nature brought her way.

Maggie relaxed next to Jenny, extending her arms along the back of the sofa. "I wasn't sure you'd like roughing it. This place is no palace."

Jenny laughed. "Good try, Conover. The truth is more likely two-fold. You weren't sure you wanted my company for a weekend and you weren't sure you were willing to share your retreat with me."

"Would it do any good to deny your reasoning?" She grinned at Jenny.

"Not really. I think I've come to know you pretty well in the past month. You're careful about committing your time," Jenny said. She felt a friendship and closeness for Maggie that she had not felt before with anyone.

"Whatever the reason," Maggie said, "I'm glad you're here now."

"Are there fireplaces in the bedrooms?"

"Yes, but one doesn't draw well. I meant to have it fixed, but it keeps slipping my mind. I closed the damper on it last winter." She took a shilling from her pocket. "I'll flip you for the room with the fireplace." She tossed the coin into the air. "You call it. Heads or tails?"

"Tails."

"Heads. I get the bedroom with the fireplace." She returned the coin to her pocket. "You get extra blankets. You won't be cold, but you won't be able to move either."

"Did anyone ever tell you that you're a real charmer?" Jenny said. She liked Maggie's playfulness.

"Not lately," Maggie said. She smiled. "But whatever I am beats freezing to death."

"I'll sleep out here in front of the fire," Jenny poked the sofa cushion to test for softness. "It seems pretty comfortable."

"Before you settle in," Maggie said, "let's take a walk on the beach."

* * * * *

The wind off the ocean felt frigid on Maggie's face. It rolled in with the waves and made its way up the deserted beach. They walked within two feet of the barbed wire, then paralleled its march across the sand. The tide was moving in quickly. Maggie watched its long gray fingers stretch further and further up the beach. They deposited lacy white foam on the tidal pools left behind. The constant rhythm made a soft rushing and breaking sound as one wave followed another with less and less space between. A flock of seagulls hovered a mile from shore, dive-bombing for their intended prey, screeching encouragement to each other to try again.

Maggie pulled the collar up on her flight jacket and pushed her hands into the warmth of her pockets. "I love this place," she said. "Given a choice, I'd take the ocean over the mountains every time." Maggie watched the water as she spoke. "Do you like the ocean, Jenny?"

Jenny's eyes were on Maggie. "Yes," she said. "It's soothing and exciting at the same time." She turned toward the sea. "It looks so peaceful, it's hard to believe that battles are going on out there."

"The destruction goes on out there just as it does on land."

"I know," Jenny said. Her voice was rich with understanding. "I've seen enough broken sailors to know that's true. I used to think I'd like to live in one place when the war is over." She turned and looked again at Maggie. "I'm not so sure about that now. I've seen enough wounded and dying people to realize how really tenuous life is." She pulled her collar up around her neck. "It can be changed or stopped in the space of a heartbeat. I want a chance to experience life." She smiled. "I seem to remember that you said almost the same thing when we first met. I didn't understand your feelings very well then, but I do now." Her face was serious. "I'm not the same person who came to England. War has killed my innocence." She flashed a fleeting smile. "I don't know whether to mourn or celebrate its passing."

"Maybe a little of both," Maggie said. She felt drawn to the new wisdom she saw in Jenny. This was a more sensitive and searching woman than the lieutenant she had met months ago. "You have your whole life ahead of you. This war is only a detour. Whatever you go through now can only add richness to your future."

"I hope you're right," Jenny said. "I'm not so sure about myself anymore." She looked directly at Maggie. "I'm afraid I don't really know myself. Maybe I'm the type who will always think of myself first. The type who will become hardened to suffering." She looked away. "I'm not sure who I am anymore. I have thoughts and feelings I hardly recognize as my own."

49

"Did your self-doubt begin with David?" She felt she was walking a tightrope.

Jenny turned toward Maggie. "He certainly doesn't help," she said. "But he's no more to blame than I am. I'm probably responsible for some of his lack of confidence."

Maggie cautioned herself not to be too blunt. The wrong word, the wrong tone, could send Jenny in the wrong direction. "I think you're being too hard on yourself. From what I saw of David, he treats you like a child. He certainly doesn't encourage you to develop your interests or talents. It amazes me that you tolerate it."

"What choice do I have? He's my husband."

The words ignited new anger in Maggie. She didn't need to be reminded of that fact. The knowledge haunted her thoughts. "I'm not the right person to answer that question. I don't like David. I'm not sure I can be unbiased."

"Right now I'm not looking for impartiality," Jenny said. Her body shivered from the cold. "Right now I could use someone who was totally on my side."

Maggie stopped the words in her mouth. She felt an overwhelming desire to take Jenny into her arms. Her eyes embraced Jenny. She realized suddenly that Jenny was trembling. "Why didn't you say you were cold?" Maggie asked. She pulled off her scarf and put it around Jenny's neck. Her hands trembled slightly as she pushed its ends inside Jenny's coat. Passion flared inside her as her hand grazed Jenny's breast. The image of Jenny's body, yielding against hers, filled her with desire, desire so intense she doubted her ability to resist. Panic gripped her. I can't give in to this, she thought. It could ruin any chance for the future. She needed to get away from Jenny for a while. "Let's go in. You can get warm in front of the fire." She glanced at her watch. "I need to leave anyway. I'm due at the USO in twenty minutes," she lied.

"I'll make dinner for us. Do you know how long you'll be?"

"I should be back by five-thirty. I'll pick up some shrimp while I'm in town. Why don't you make a salad to go with them?"

CHAPTER 7

Jenny stood in front of the fire. When she was warm, she changed into slacks and a sweater.

Maggie was right, she thought. This bedroom is cold. Hanging her uniform in the small closet, she noticed several blankets on the shelf above the clothes rack. As she pulled the bottom blanket toward her, several photographs fell from the shelf and landed at her feet.

Maggie was in all three photos. In two she was standing with her arm around the shoulders of an attractive Royal Air Force sergeant. The woman was taller than Maggie, with light, shoulder-length hair. The remaining photo showed Maggie, the sergeant, and Christine. She turned the photos over and read the few words scribbled on their backs. "Ann and Maggie — February 1942." "Maggie, Sis and me — Christmas 1941."

Jenny studied the photos. One showed Maggie's eyes clearly on Ann, her face soft and filled with love. The inscription read, "To Maggie — All My Love — All My Life — Ann — Xmas 1941."

Jenny was filled with a strong, undeniable jealously and an intense dislike for this woman who had captured Maggie's heart. I wonder why they were removed from the mantel, she thought. Maybe they broke up. She found the thought comforting.

She stretched out on the sofa and spread the blanket over her. She looked at the photos again. They've probably kissed a hundred times, she thought. Long, passionate kisses. Jealousy burned inside her. She took a deep breath and closed her eyes. She didn't want to think of Maggie with Ann. She didn't want to think of Maggie with anyone. Still . . .

She ran her fingers across her lips. She saw Maggie leaning toward her, her blue eyes alive with love and passion. Maggie's lips hungry for her. A wave of excitement washed through her. She surrendered to Maggie's mouth.

A second image filled her mind. Maggie's hands, graceful and tender, moving over her naked breasts. She felt her nipples grow erect as she offered herself to Maggie. She felt her body shiver as she melted into Maggie's hands.

This is ridiculous. She tossed the photographs onto the coffee table, laid back and closed her eyes. No more crazy thoughts, she told herself. Maggie is my friend.

The warmth of the fire moved into the room and wrapped itself around her. It caressed her face and lulled her into sleep. Images of Maggie lay down beside her and followed her into dreams.

She sensed Maggie's presence before she felt her touch. Her satiny lips brushed against her mouth — gentle, tasting of new rain. Maggie smiled down at her. She closed her eyes and felt Maggie's mouth, more insistent now, more passionate in her kiss. Her lips opened to Maggie's tongue as her breathing grew more rapid. Passion and desire claimed her for their own.

"Jenny." Maggie's voice was soft and dreamlike. She felt a cool touch on her cheek. She opened her eyes and looked sleepily at Maggie. Her dark blue eyes were warm and intense, and there, just beneath the surface, the kiss still lingered.

"Have I been asleep that long?" She sat up and rubbed her eyes. "I haven't made our salad. I was going to relax for ten minutes." She looked at her watch. "That was two hours ago."

"That's okay," Maggie said. "We can make one now."

* * * * *

They ate dinner in front of the fire, cleared the dishes, and straightened the kitchen together.

"I'd forgotten how good fresh shrimp can taste," Jenny said. She leaned against the back of the sofa. "You're a good cook."

"I like to cook," Maggie said. "It relaxes me." She picked up the photographs from the coffee table and looked through them slowly. "Where did you find these?" Her eyes were riveted on the photos.

"They fell when I got the blanket from the closet shelf." Jenny leaned forward and looked at the pictures again. "She's very pretty."

"She was. She was killed more than a year ago," Maggie said.

Maggie's face was the color of chalk, her eyes glazed with tears. Sorrow spread across Maggie's face as Jenny reached for her hand. "I didn't mean to trigger unhappy memories for you," Jenny said. "Would it help if you talked about it?"

She felt Maggie's eyes penetrate her. She's searching for something, Jenny thought. Dear God, let her find it in me. She squeezed Maggie's hand. "I'm a good listener." Tell me, she thought.

Maggie looked away. Jenny could see the tension in Maggie's throat where the muscles twitched as Maggie swallowed her tears.

She reached for and took Maggie's hand. She could feel the unseen tremor of Maggie's pain. "Please Maggie, let me help. Tell me what's hurt you so."

In the fraction of a second all defenses vanished from Maggie's eyes. Jenny felt the gift of total trust and vulnerability. She accepted it.

"I was responsible for Ann's death," Maggie said. Her face and voice were heavy with agony. "If it

wasn't for me, Ann would be alive today." Tears
streamed down Maggie's cheeks "Ann and I were
lovers. I know most people can't understand that.
That they'd see us as sick and perverted. But we
were in love." Her eyes brightened with memory. "We
spent every moment we could together. Every moment
the war and my career would allow." She glanced
down, new tears beginning their way along her
cheeks. "I loved one thing more than Ann. My work.
It came before anything else. When I had a chance
for an assignment I had wanted for months, I jumped
at it. It didn't matter that Ann and I had plans for
that weekend. I insisted that she trade her weekend
off, work that weekend, and plan on Brighton the
following week. She was pretty angry. It was the
fourth time that month I'd cancelled our plans
because of work."

Jenny could feel the pain — razor-sharp in
Maggie.

"There wasn't another weekend." Maggie closed
her eyes and bit her lip, her face flushed. She spoke
between sobs. "While I was off taking care of my
career, the Germans bombed the air base. Ann was
killed trying to reach her duty station." She snapped
her fingers. "Just like that, she was gone. A German
plane strafed the field." She ran her hand across her
forehead with obvious disbelief. *"One* piece of
shrapnel hit her." She held up her index finger.
"One." Her voice broke and she wept her words into
the room. "It tore her heart to shreds."

Jenny felt her own tears as she wrapped her arms
around Maggie and drew her close. "My poor
Maggie." She brushed her lips against Maggie's soft

curls. "It's not your fault." She closed her arms tighter. "You didn't cause her death."

Maggie pulled back and looked at Jenny. Her face was a torrent of tears. "I did, Jenny. It was my fault. If I hadn't asked her to trade weekends, she'd still be alive."

Jenny wiped Maggie's tears with her hand. More than anything in the world, she wanted to soothe Maggie. Her heart ached with the desire to comfort her, the need to express her desire.

She held Maggie's face between her hands and looked deeply into her eyes. "Listen to me, Maggie, I've seen a lot of pain and a lot of dying. I've asked myself a thousand times, with a hundred different patients, what I could have done differently to save a patient's life. If I'd given an injection a minute sooner, walked into a room ten seconds earlier, or worked straight through instead of stopping for coffee. If I'd done any one of those, would my patient have lived?" She brushed the tears from Maggie's cheeks. "I don't know. But I do know that I cared about those people. That I didn't want even one of them to die. Could I have done more? Maybe. But I can't go back and do it over. Not even God can change the past."

She smoothed the curls from Maggie's forehead. "What it finally comes down to is so simple, it's easy to overlook. My pain didn't stop until I accepted the fact that I'm not perfect. That like it or not, I'm human. I can't fix everything. And no matter how badly I want to, I can't solve everyone's problems, or cure everyone's sickness." She looked into Maggie's eyes. "When I forgave myself for not being God, for being human, and when I forgave the patients who

57

had died despite my efforts to save them, the sharpness of the pain went away. Not completely. But enough to let me live in peace with myself." She ran her hand across Maggie's cheeks. "Don't you think it's time to forgive yourself for being human, to forgive Ann for dying? Haven't you carried this long enough? I'm absolutely certain that a woman who loved you enough to share your life, loved you enough to want you to be happy."

Tension drained from Maggie's face. Her arms closed around Jenny and she whispered, "It's time I tried."

CHAPTER 8

David telephoned before boarding a plane for Debden Air Base. A German air attack had put his ship in dry dock for repairs. He would be in London for three days and had managed to borrow a flat from a friend. He gave Jenny the address and told her where to pick up the key.

She was waiting when David arrived. "I'm glad you weren't hurt," Jenny said as he released her from a rough embrace.

"Did you get a pass?" He sat down on the worn brown sofa and motioned for Jenny to join him.

"I don't have to be back until Monday," Jenny said. "I already had a pass. I was planning to go to Brighton for the weekend."

"We can still go if you have a room there," David said. He glanced around the tiny flat. "This place is dismal."

Jenny was annoyed with David's ingratitude. "I think it was nice of your friend to lend it to you."

She looked around the room. It was crowded with old furniture. The upholstered pieces were either sagging or showing the worn outline of springs. Everything else was chipped, marred or broken.

"I didn't have a room," Jenny said. "I was invited by a friend to stay at her cottage." Disappointed, she remembered her plans with Maggie.

David stood and walked to the bedroom doorway. "God," he said, "the bed looks worse than the rest of the furniture." He reclaimed his place on the sofa. "Do you think your friend would lend the cottage to us? It has to be better than this place."

"She has company this weekend," Jenny said. "She'll be using it herself." Anger flashed at the thought of David in the cottage. He doesn't belong there, she thought. It's our place. Mine and Maggie's.

"Just my luck to have a hen party rob me of a weekend at the shore." He sounded sorry for himself. "The way things have been going for the past month, I might as well not exist. It's as if my ideas and feelings don't count. Somebody, somewhere, has a plan for my life, and I don't get a choice." His whining was irritating. "I'm sure not treated like a man."

His words assaulted her. That's exactly how he treats me, she thought. She took a good look at her husband. His face wore the pout of a selfish child, as always when he didn't get his way.

"You wouldn't believe what I went through last week," David said. His voice had a "poor me" tone. "To begin with, in the first minute of their run Gerry kills my best gunner. The kid was no prize, but he did hit what he aimed at most of the time. His back-up takes five minutes to hit one damned plane. By then, the flight deck was torn up pretty badly. All our aircraft are out so we have to work our asses off to get it in shape so the flyboys can land."

Jenny wanted to shake David. To make him hear how his whining sounded. How different he is from Maggie, she thought. He's only concerned with how something affects him. She had never liked this trait in David. She hated it now.

"And that's not the worst of it," David continued, indignant. "We were transporting twenty British Sisters to a hospital ship. Replacements. We were to rendezvous with the ship and transfer the Sisters on board. We never got them there. A bomb hit their section of the ship, tore the hell out of everything. Including them. Nineteen killed. The one who's alive lost both legs. She's lucky in a way. Could have been her face."

He looked at Jenny intently. "Would you believe the Captain chewed my ass out for not moving them to an inside section when the attack started? Hell, I told them when they came on board, If the ship comes under attack, move to Section Six-B. It's not my fault if they were too stupid to listen. I'm not going to become a target trying to rescue women who can't think under pressure. I intend to stay out of

61

the line of fire whenever possible, and to survive this war in one piece."

Shocked at David's callousness, she said, "I'm sure they didn't want to die." She could feel her anger creep into her tone.

"No. And the one who got her legs blown off didn't want that either." David's face twisted into a sneer. "She's a married woman. How do you think her husband is going to feel coming home to that? Think he'll want her now? I saw my uncle's life ruined by a crippled wife. His whole life fell apart. Career, home, everything. He ended up committing suicide."

David had moved beyond Jenny's ability to hold her anger inside. Disgusted, she could no longer be silent. "You sound like a cold, selfish monster. Don't you feel anything for those women? Is their death just an inconvenience in your life?"

David's face reddened. "I'll tell you who I feel sorry for," he responded. "That cripple's husband. They've been married six months, and he can look forward to a future with a freak." His face grew grim with determination. "That's not going to happen to me. You're going to resign your commission and move to the country until this war is over."

Jenny was furious. Millions of brave men and women had risked their lives for freedom. Thousands had died. Tens of thousands would forever bear war's scars. "You pompous ass." She flung her words at David like a rock. "How dare you make light of the suffering of other people. Even an animal grieves for the death of its kind."

"Who do you think you're talking to? I'm your husband." David's face was almost purple. His eyes were slits. "No girl talks to me like that. Least of all my wife. You'll do as I tell you, and I'm telling you to resign. I'm not about to drag some cripple around for the rest of my life. You'll eventually get sent on a landing somewhere. I don't care what the Army may tell you, a combat zone is never really secure. Aid stations get bombed all the time. So do the hospital ships. Hundreds of Sisters and doctors have been killed and even more have been scarred and mangled."

He slammed his fist against the arm of the sofa. "I've told you I'm going to leave this war alive and in one piece. I'm not going to be a dead hero."

His words tore through her mind like a bullet. "My God, you're not callous, you're a coward!"

For the first time genuine pity mingled with her hatred for David. How could she have missed this before? It all added up now — the bullying, the callous remarks, the insistence that he control everything. All to hide his cowardice. All worthy of her pity and contempt.

CHAPTER 9

The three days Jenny spent with David were almost unbearable. He vacillated between badgering her to leave the service, criticizing her friendship with Maggie, and wanting to make love.

"You're my wife," David yelled. "You're obligated to go to bed with me."

"I can't argue one minute and make love the next," Jenny shouted. "I need to feel close to you first."

"Bull," David said. His eyes were narrow slits of anger. "You made love before without feeling close to me. What's different now?" He leaned across the bed and glared at her.

Jenny met his eyes. "I'm different," she said. Her voice was calm. "I'm not going through the motions anymore. If we make love it will be because we both want it."

He reached for Jenny's shoulders and pulled her to him. "Is that so?" He spit the words at her. "I could force you. No one would say I was wrong."

Jenny felt her determination grow. "I'd say you were wrong," she said. "Do you really believe we could build a marriage on rape? That's what it would be, you know. It wouldn't be love."

David threw her back against her pillow and stood up. "Is that what your queer friend told you? She's certainly the one to give advice on marriage." His face was ugly with anger and hate. "I'll bet she's never had a man in her life."

"Leave Maggie out of this. She's never done one thing to hurt you." She was furious at him. "Maggie's private life is her business. She doesn't flaunt it, and she doesn't talk to me about it. Whether she's sleeping with men, or women, is none of your business."

"It is if it involves my wife," David bullied. He gathered his words to himself like a battle flag, a rallying point for his attacks. "Any man would tell you the same thing."

"I don't give a damn what your buddies think." Jenny felt the assurance that comes with defending a friend. "Maggie Conover is a sensitive, caring woman. We're friends, David. Nothing more. And I don't intend to give up her friendship for your dirty mind."

That night he forced himself on her. Cold sober, with deliberate intent. She screamed at him at first until her screams melted into silent tears. An icy hand moved against everything inside her, numbing her completely.

When he finished she pushed him off her and got into the shower. The warm water brought some feeling back. Her thighs and stomach hurt from the force of David's attack. Her wrists were sore and bruised. She felt herself sinking into depression as long deep sobs filled her throat and mouth. I'll never feel clean again, she thought.

She spent the night in a bedroom chair. Fully dressed and awake, she listened to the sounds of David's sleep. He turned onto his back and began to snore.

The pain in her stomach was worse. She shifted her position in the chair. What a pitiful coward he was. Depression numbed her thoughts as she waited for morning.

He seemed embarrassed as he dressed. Jenny said as little as possible to him. They ate breakfast in cold, almost total, silence.

He kissed her on the cheek before leaving for his ship. She turned away from him completely.

CHAPTER 10

Jenny was afraid she was losing her mind. Thoughts of David and Maggie pushed themselves into her crowded days, and intruded into her dreams. She worked by rote while at the hospital, using her training and sheer determination to do and say the right things. The right thing had been second nature to her since her early childhood. Now, in a foreign country, in the midst of war, her view of what was right was fading before her eyes. She no longer had a black and white picture of what was correct. Feelings she managed to ignore before returned with new strength and changed her focus on the world.

David's actions had forced her to look at the bankruptcy of their marriage. What feeling she had for him was negative. There's nothing left to be committed to, she thought. A ceremony and a piece of paper aren't enough to create a marriage. She knew how disappointed her parents would be if she separated from David, how miserable she'd be if she didn't. Thank God she didn't have to make the decision now.

But her marriage was only part of the conflict. Her feelings for Maggie were too strong to ignore any longer. Her conclusion shook her to the core. I'm in love with her, she thought. How could this happen? I've lived all my life with the knowledge I'd marry and have children.

She felt tiny beads of perspiration as they formed on her forehead and upper lip. She couldn't want her sexually. It wasn't normal to feel this way.

She walked to the window of her office and looked out into the cold November day. The sky was gray and fuzzy. Fog hung close to the sidewalks, hiding the feet of passersby. Two young women were moving toward the corner. Both wore American Army uniforms with the rank of Lieutenant. Both were attractive, with long dark hair, and warm friendly smiles. At the corner, one turned to check the seams on her stockings. Her skirt rose slightly as she moved a seam closer to mid-center. Her legs were thin and shapely with narrow ankles. See, she thought, I don't feel attracted to her. She's pretty and I don't feel a thing.

No sooner had the thought entered her mind than a picture of Maggie followed behind it, lingering, claiming her full attention. Maggie's face was smiling at her. She could see it as clearly as if Maggie were in the room. Her short blonde curls looked like corn silk and her deep blue eyes were kind and understanding. Jenny could see the dimple on each cheek as Maggie laughed, a deep rich laugh that reminded her of a child. She remembered the touch of Maggie's hand against her skin, and desire raced through her. She wanted to feel Maggie's touch again. To run her fingers against her hand. She held her breath as she imagined the soft touch of Maggie's lips against her mouth. She trembled as imaginary arms closed around her and the touch of Maggie's body pressed inch for inch against her own.

This is wrong, she thought. Taking pleasure in these thoughts was a mortal sin. She wished she could talk to a psychiatrist. She ran her hand through her hair and began to pace. That won't work, she thought. A psychiatrist would have to turn her in as a security risk. She could talk to a priest but she knew what a priest would say.

She looked out the window again. If Maggie were here, she'd try to help.

As if attached to Maggie's name, warm feelings flooded her awareness. Christine, she thought. She could talk to Christine. She had to know her sister was involved with Maggie. She must have some understanding of these feelings. She would talk to her.

CHAPTER 11

Christine's flat was neat and clean. Bookcases lined an entire wall. On the end table, the coffee table, and the server, books were arranged in neat, even stacks. The furniture wasn't new, but it was well cared for.

"Thank you for letting me come over." Jenny seated herself on the floral-patterned sofa and looked at Christine. It was the first time she had seen her in civilian clothes. The dark green sweater and light gray slacks emphasized her trim figure. She looked softer without the formality of her uniform and the insignia of rank.

"Can I get you something? A soft drink or a cup of tea?"

"No, thank you." Jenny was tense.

Christine sat opposite her. "You sounded upset on the phone. What can I do to help?"

"I'm not entirely sure." She watched Christine's face closely. Maybe it was a mistake to come here. After all, she wasn't positive that Christine had accepted Ann and Maggie. What if she hadn't? I could be letting myself in for a verbal beating, Jenny thought. Even if she won't turn me in, she may resent my feelings. After all, she and Maggie are like ex-sisters-in-law.

"Maggie told me about her relationship with Ann," Jenny said suddenly. "It must have been a shock for you to learn they were involved."

For a minute Christine didn't respond. Jenny guessed she was weighing whether to be honest or guarded, or both.

"I'm surprised Maggie mentioned it to you," Christine said cautiously. "It's not something one usually discusses in everyday conversation." She leaned back in her chair and crossed her arms.

Jenny filled Christine in about her discovery of the pictures. "Ann must have been very special." She watched Christine's face grow soft, her eyes become tender.

"She was," Christine said. "She was an extremely kind and loyal person. I didn't approve of her relationship with Maggie, but I accepted it." Her eyes looked distant for a second. "I would have preferred to see Ann married with a family. I told both of them

71

that. We were honest with each other." She unfolded her arms. "I was able to accept their relationship when I realized they really were in love. There is no other reason I can see for taking the risk such a relationship involves. Maggie has become a good friend. I love her dearly." Christine's gaze was a statement and a question.

Jenny made her decision. She would confide in Christine, but remain cautious. "I'm in love with Maggie," she said. It was the first time she had spoken the words out loud. The first time she had declared her love for Maggie to another human being. Their sound and meaning washed over her like a wave. She felt the truth of her words take root in her heart.

Christine looked stunned. She was staring at Jenny in obvious shock. "I'm not sure what to say," Christine replied. "I've encouraged Maggie to find someone, but I don't think I ever thought about it concretely. She's belonged to Ann and me for a long time."

Jenny heard the jealousy in Christine's voice. "I don't want to take Ann's place. I'm sure she'll always have a special place in Maggie's heart. I understand that." She paused. "I'm jealous sometimes, but I understand it." She looked directly into Christine's eyes. "I know this must be hard for you, but you're the only person I felt fairly sure would not turn me in to the military."

"No. I won't do that," Christine said. "But I'm not sure I'll welcome you with open arms either." She folded her arms again and tilted her head to one side. "I don't know you yet. I don't know what you want from Maggie, whether you're serious about her

72

or just curious. I've seen a few curious women go after her before. They, as you Americans say, never reached first base."

Jenny felt slightly defensive. "In my case I'm afraid you're way ahead of me. I haven't even told Maggie how I feel. I'm afraid that I know absolutely nothing about a homosexual relationship. I've never even been attracted to a woman before. Actually, I'm not overjoyed to be in love with a woman now. It seems an impossibly difficult road. For one thing, I don't even know if Maggie feels the same way. I think she does, but I'm not sure. Then there's the matter of my marriage. It exists on paper now, but I know the seriousness of divorce. I know it's looked on by society as a major failure in a person's life. I can't say the idea of being a divorced woman is a happy one for me."

"Hmp." Christine shifted her position and crossed her legs. "If you think society frowns on divorce, it's nothing compared to how it feels about homosexuality." She took a deep breath. "Ann and Maggie went through some rough times. There were several times when rumors about them had to be dealt with. That kind of rumor can ruin an entire life."

"I know. Sometimes I think I'm crazy for even considering such a thing. I can think of many reasons I shouldn't." She felt increasing trust for Christine.

"There's only one reason to consider it, Jenny." Christine's face and voice softened. "If you really love each other, it could be worth the risks. I saw a rare closeness between Ann and Maggie. It was as if they were truly part of each other. As if each had fallen in love with her best friend and gone right on being best friends."

Jenny pushed a tinge of jealousy out of her mind. "I think I know what you mean," she said. "I really appreciate your time and your opinion. You've helped a lot." She looked at her watch. "I'm due at a meeting in forty minutes. I appreciate your willingness to talk with me."

Christine nodded. "I'm willing to listen any time. I can only promise to try to be unbiased."

Jenny stood and extended her hand. "Thank you. That sounds like a fair beginning."

CHAPTER 12

Maggie was finally on a bomber heading for Germany. She had fought hard for the right to accompany a bomber crew on a mission. The Eighth Air Force had refused several requests with the rationale that it was far too dangerous for a woman. The Royal Air Force accepted Maggie's argument that a bombing mission couldn't be more dangerous than living in London during the Blitz.

She sat on a metal seat near the middle gunner. The clear plastic blister that allowed the gunner to watch for enemy planes gave her a perfect view of the perimeter track and the main runway. The quiet night air came alive as two hundred Lancaster bombers started their engines. Maggie, excited and awed, watched the dark silhouettes ahead of her roll slowly along the track, race down the runway, and disappear into the cold night sky. Finally, it was time for her ship, Prince of Wales, to take off. Inertia pulled her backward as the huge plane climbed into the darkness above. She breathed a sigh of relief as the ship took its place in the formation. They couldn't change their minds now. She had been plagued by the fear that before Prince of Wales was airborne someone would decide she shouldn't be on board, and the plane would taxi to the hangar area and wait for her to get off. Now it was too late. Prince of Wales was committed, and Maggie was an official observer.

She pulled herself erect, the weight of the parachute heavy against her shoulders, and looked around the cavernous belly of the plane. It was large but had very little living space. The bomb bay in the center of its belly was surrounded by a metal elliptical catwalk. The navigator sat at a small desk to Maggie's far left. Just above her head, his feet clearly visible, the mid-gunner sat in his turret, his eyes pinned on the sky. Frank Ames, the young man directly across from her, had been friendly during the two days of her orientation to the base and the ship. His friendly blue eyes had now lost all hint of a smile. He was watching the sky closely.

The vibration of the motors under the metal floor caused her feet and legs to tingle slightly. She knew from her orientation that there would be little time for chitchat. Even conversation over the plane's

76

intercom was kept at a minimum. A plane in a bombardment group took every pair of eyes to keep it at a safe distance from the other one hundred and ninety-nine planes that surrounded it. Maggie had been told of several instances where two Lancs had come together accidentally with explosions so intense that even the smallest pieces could not be seen. Maggie shivered as the meaning of that sunk into her mind. For an instant, without warning, she saw Jenny's face smiling at her. A warm exhilaration flowed through her as she thought about sharing this mission with Jenny. The plane rose and fell quickly as it passed the air stream of one of the unseen Lancs up ahead. Maggie's stomach churned with the unexpected movement.

"On course and on time." The navigator, Neil Blackburn, spoke into the intercom.

"Roger. Is everyone doing all right?" The pilot's voice floated into the compartment. "How's our passenger?"

"She looks fine," Neil Blackburn said. He smiled at Maggie.

Maggie listened as the pilot checked with the tail gunner. "I'm doing fine, Jim." The young man's voice was crisp and alive.

Maggie strained to see into the darkness. The planes were flying without running lights. An added danger, she thought. She could barely make out the dim dark lines that traced their shapes against the blackness.

"Searchlight band up ahead," the navigator said. "Mark for position."

Maggie looked down and saw a wide beam of moving light. As they got closer she could distinguish smaller, narrower bands inside. Each moving frantically, searching for intruders. She was relieved that they remained outside the band of light, which disappeared off the wing as the giant engines pulled them closer to the target.

What a lucky break, Maggie thought, to pull Berlin as the target on my first flight.

"More searchlights ahead." Neil Blackburn's voice interrupted her thoughts.

Beams of light rose into the sky from the ground below the right wing tip. Like long graceful fingers, they sifted the night air for any sign of allied planes.

"My God," Maggie said, "how could any plane get through that?" Her mouth was dry as she wiped perspiration from her forehead. For the first time since the mission began, she was afraid. She knew with certainty that she did not want to fly into that glaring splotch of light.

"Some make it," the bomb aimer said. "We don't have to try. It's not our target."

Maggie relaxed a little, but was unable to take her eyes off the giant swatch of searchlights. She felt more comfortable as the glare faded, slowly disappearing into the past as Prince of Wales moved forward — ever closer to Berlin.

For almost an hour there were no lights visible on the ground. The crew was busy and quiet. Neil Blackburn was constantly checking his maps and compass. The bomb aimer and mid-gunner sat at semi-attention as they peered into the darkness for friend or foe. Maggie leaned against the metal seat, lulled by the soft blackness that surrounded her and the hum of the motors that sang continuously in her ears.

Prince of Wales lurched upward as it crossed the wake of another Lanc.

"Target dead ahead," Blackburn said, his voice calm and strong.

Maggie peered out, anxious for her first glimpse of Berlin. There was no sight of light. Somewhere down there, she thought, Adolf Hitler is plotting the destruction of freedom. It was hard to believe one megalomaniac could lead an entire nation into war and atrocities. She shivered as the thought of Hitler's plan to annihilate the Jews passed through her mind. But it's more than the Jews, she thought, remembering her conversations with several journalists who had escaped Nazi hands. He's killed thousands of people just for being different. Jews, cripples, and homosexuals had been murdered in Nazi concentration camps. She might have shared the same end had she been born in Germany — a sobering thought.

"Coming up over target," Blackburn said.

The bomb aimer was bent over the site known as Oboe, an American invention shared with her British allies.

The pilot's voice was clear. "You have control, Frank. Put them down the Fuhrer's throat."

"Will do," Frank Ames said. He never moved his eyes from the bomb site.

Maggie wondered about the people on the ground. The air-raid sirens must be screaming in the city. How many people had managed to take cover? There wasn't one light down there. Maybe the navigator had made a mistake.

As she was considering the possibility, lights appeared everywhere. They shot up from the ground like the long arms of sea monsters, flailing across the sky, hunting the British attackers. Maggie's heart was racing now, pounding hard against her chest. Fear returned as cold terror.

"Bomb bay open," Frank Ames said.

Maggie could see huge Christmas trees of red and green lights below them. She remembered that these were the target markers dropped by the Pathfinders. Small explosions of white light flared on the ground. The flight had started its run. She was hypnotized by the thousands of incendiary bombs setting Berlin on fire. Then it was their turn. Prince of Wales slowed slightly, then jumped upward.

"Incendiaries away," the bomb aimer said.

Bursts of ack-ack assaulted her ears. The sky exploded in bright puffs all around them.

Suddenly the tail gunner's voice shot into the intercom. "Fighters coming up at five o'clock," he called. "Corkscrew. Corkscrew."

The pilot took control, rolling the plane to its left and beginning a spiralling descent.

Maggie was thrown against the bulkhead. She felt her stomach rise to her throat. Dear God, she thought, don't let me die before I see Jenny again.

Prince of Wales leveled out and resumed its normal course. "It's all yours, Frank," the pilot said.

"Roger. Beginning second run," the bomb aimer replied. Again his eyes were glued to Oboe.

Maggie felt the ship lurch upward as if something heavy had fallen from its belly.

"Block Buster gone," the bomb aimer said. "You have control."

The pilot began an immediate turn and Prince of Wales took its place in the waiting formation.

Berlin was a solid sheet of flames. Maggie was awed as she considered the dreadful power the Lancasters had carried to Hitler's own city.

"We're going home," the pilot said.

The burning city appeared on the other side of the plane. Maggie could see red tracers as they streaked into the night sky — thin hot streamers of steel promising destruction and death to whatever lay in their path. She wanted to hurry Prince of Wales through the night. Urgency to escape Berlin's air space combined with her fear. She could see her fear echoed in the faces of the crew. They weren't out of danger. Why couldn't they move faster?

The intercom crackled, and the tail gunner's voice shot out of it. "Fighters at eleven o'clock. Corkscrew. Corkscrew."

The pilot rolled the plane to the right and began another spiralling descent. It was too late. Hot steel ripped into the mid-turret blister. Cold air and something sharp slapped into Maggie's forehead, stunning her. She fell backward, the hardness of the steel deck against her back and left shoulder. Something warm was running into her left eye. She touched her forehead. Blood, she thought. I'm cut. The plane leveled out and the pilot's voice came over the intercom. "Is everyone all right? How much damage did we get?"

Maggie stood and steadied herself against the bulkhead. Cold air had turned the belly of the Lancaster into an ice box.

"We're hit pretty bad. They took out the mid-blister," Neil Blackburn said. "Frank and Bobbie are down. Let me check them and get back to you."

"I'll check Bobbie," Maggie said. "You check Frank." She moved quickly to the young gunner. He was sprawled belly down against the steel deck. Maggie was running on raw energy. She turned him over slowly, pulling his shoulders toward her. "Oh God," she said, "he has no face." She felt her stomach muscles contract and for an instant, thought she would vomit.

"Is he dead?" Neil Blackburn called across the cabin. "Check his heart."

Maggie looked at the man's chest. A large ragged hole had opened him like a can of beans. She could see his heart lying still inside a pool of blood. She fought the need to be sick. "He's dead," she said.

Blackburn was talking to the pilot again. "Frank and Bobbie are dead. Conover has a deep gash in her forehead. I'm hit in the arm and losing blood fast. I'll get Conover to help with a tourniquet. Can we keep up with the Group? I may pass out. You'll need to follow them home."

"We can keep up. As soon as you have the tourniquet on, check on Mike. He doesn't answer."

Maggie was tying the tourniquet in place when Neil Blackburn folded and collapsed on the deck.

"Neil?" the pilot said. "Can you hear me?"

"He's unconscious," Maggie called. "I'll check on Mike."

"Thanks, Conover," the pilot said. "You're all right."

She took the box of medical supplies with her and found the tail gunner hanging sideways out of his chair. Blood covered the front of his shirt. She unbuckled the straps that held him in place and pulled his body to the deck. She opened his shirt, poured sulfa on his wounds, and covered them with a sterile bandage.

"Conover, is he alive?" the pilot asked.

"Yes," Maggie said. "Hurt but alive." There was a loud gurgling sound, and the man began to choke. Maggie reached for the First Aid kit.

"What's wrong, Conover?" the pilot said.

"He's choking. I'm going to do a trach," Maggie said. She felt his throat for the firm rings of cartilage that gave his airway shape. She cut between the rings and pushed a small rubber tube into the incision.

"You know how to do a trach?" the pilot asked incredulously.

"I've done one before. During an air raid in the Blitz," Maggie said. She was aware that her head hurt. "Besides, it's done. He's stopped choking."

Maggie dragged the tail gunner to the plane's belly. She untied the tourniquet on Neil's arm, waited, and retied it.

When they landed at their base the pilot walked back to Maggie. "Good show, Conover. You should have been British."

Maggie was too tired to feel anything. She wanted to sleep.

CHAPTER 13

"What happened to your head?" Jenny said. She put her arms around Maggie and hugged her.

"I'll tell you on our way to Brighton." She steered Jenny to the car.

Driving, she watched Jenny out of the corner of her eye as she related the bombing mission to her.

"How awful," Jenny said. She reached out and rested her hand on Maggie's thigh. "I'm really glad you're back."

Maggie could feel the heat and pressure of Jenny's palm. Desire carried the heat of promise throughout her body. She glanced at Jenny and returned her eyes quickly to the road. The thought of Jenny's mouth conjured up an erotic fantasy. Passion stirred below as she felt her mouth on Jenny's. She wanted to say the words out loud — tell Jenny how much she loved her, how much she wanted her. Not now, she thought. It's not the time.

* * * * *

Maggie replaced the fire screen and sat down next to Jenny.

"The fire's beautiful," Jenny said. She turned her face toward Maggie. For an instant the two gazed into each other's eyes. Maggie was overcome with love and desire for Jenny. When she reached out and brushed the strands of hair from Jenny's forehead, it was warm between her fingers, and she fought to control her desire. She could not remember when she had wanted someone more.

"You look so deep in thought," Jenny said. She covered Maggie's hand with her own. "Tell me what you're feeling."

Maggie was acutely aware of Jenny's touch. She looked down at the slim delicate hand and thought it was beautiful. The skin was fair and soft as satin. She lifted Jenny's hand to her mouth, and kissed it gently. "I need to talk to you, Jenny." She watched Jenny closely as she threaded her fingers through Jenny's. Tension gripped Jenny's face, but she didn't withdraw so much as a millimeter. Her dark brown eyes met Maggie's directly. Her lips looked moist and full.

Tell her, Maggie thought, you may not have another chance. "Jenny, I . . ." The words caught in her throat. She was falling now, spinning into Jenny's eyes, reaching out and tracing Jenny's cheek with her fingertips. Caution replaced the tension in Jenny's eyes. On fire with the need to feel Jenny against her skin, she could barely whisper, "I'm in love with you, Jenny. Head over heels." She imagined herself melting into Jenny, disappearing into Jenny's soul.

Jenny's fingers tightened against Maggie's hand. A tear rolled slowly down her cheek. "I'm so glad, Maggie," she said. She smiled tenderly. "I wanted to tell you the same thing." Her face softened. "I love you, Maggie. I never dreamed I could feel this way about a woman. But I do. I'm in love with you. I've dreamed a hundred times about your kiss, your touch . . ."

Thrilled and delighted, Maggie leaned forward and kissed Jenny's lips. They were soft and trembling as she explored them with her tongue, tracing their outline with care, returning to their fullness, brushing her tongue gently against their surfaces. Her passion flared as she felt the muscles in Jenny's back tighten. Slowly, she told herself. Slow and gentle. She nudged Jenny's lips with the tip of her tongue, and they opened willingly, inviting her inside. Waves of excitement surged through her as Jenny's tongue matched her rhythm perfectly.

Jenny's breasts pressed against her own as she ran her fingers along the back of Jenny's neck. Her body trembled as she increased the pressure of her mouth on Jenny's. The strength of her passion filled

Maggie with exhilaration. She fought her urgent need to feel Jenny's body, full-length and naked. She has to know how special she is, Maggie thought. She has to know this is more than sex. Maggie slid her hand to Jenny's breast as her mouth nibbled her lips and tongue. She opened Jenny's blouse as her mouth trailed kisses down her neck. Maggie pushed the blouse from her shoulders and unfastened the clasp on her bra. Jenny gasped as Maggie took the nipple between her fingertips, rolling it gently, delighting in its changes as it grew rigid and erect.

She pulled the clothes free and covered Jenny's breasts with slow, tender kisses. Her tongue caressed the waiting nipples, drawing lazy circles against their tips, taking them one at a time into her mouth, holding each firmly against her teeth, massaging them with her lips and tongue.

Jenny squirmed and made a low purring sound. She pushed her fingers through Maggie's hair, caressing and guiding her head, urging Maggie's mouth more firmly against herself.

Maggie slid her hand beneath Jenny's skirt, inching slowly along her inner thigh, running her fingers against the thin silk layer of cloth that covered Jenny's secret places. Jenny moaned, trembling as Maggie slipped her index and middle fingers beneath the elastic and moved inward to the slippery satin that greeted her. Love and passion consumed her as she traced the edge of desire's well and explored the firmness of the pearl. Her fingers glided along its heated head and stem, and she could hear Jenny's soft purring blend with the crackling of the fire. She unfastened the clasp on Jenny's skirt.

"No," Jenny cried. "Please, Maggie, stop." Her words were muffled by her sobs. Jenny pulled Maggie to her.

"I love you," Jenny wept. "But I can't do this."

Tenderly, Maggie enfolded Jenny in her arms.

"It's all right, Jenny." Maggie kissed the softness of her hair. "I love you." She drew Jenny closer, comforting her like a frightened child. "It's all right."

The trembling stopped and Jenny's body was still against Maggie. The clean fragrance of Jenny's hair and skin wove its way through her senses.

"I'm sorry Maggie," Jenny said, her voice filled with pain. "I should never have said anything to you. I shouldn't have told you how I feel."

Jenny's words sliced through her like a knife. She looked into Jenny's eyes. "I'm glad you told me. I wouldn't change that."

"What's wrong with me, Maggie?" New tears were beginning their way down her face. "I feel as if I'm being pulled apart inside. For the first time in my life everything I feel is against everything I've been taught. I'm at war with myself and I'm not even sure who the enemy is." Her voice was a clear whisper. "I'm in love with you, Maggie." She paused. "I feel everything those words suggest."

Wiping her tears with her hand she continued, "I keep hearing David talking about perversion. About this being unnatural. I know what people would say if they knew." She wiped her face again. "I know I shouldn't care what people think, but I do. I don't seem able to help myself. I care what my church says. I don't want to go to hell." She sobbed again, eyes rivers of tears that melted Maggie's heart. "It's already too late. I could go to hell for wanting you so much."

Maggie's mind stumbled beneath the pain of helplessness. Broken hearted, spilling love in all directions, she closed her eyes, determined to swallow her tears. They stung her throat and, in the end, they betrayed her anyway.

"I love you, Jenny. I don't want you to do anything you're not comfortable with." She held Jenny's face gently between her hands. "If it's meant to happen, it will. Next week, next month, or next year. The important thing is that nothing will happen unless you feel it's right for you."

CHAPTER 14

The remainder of the weekend was a mixture of delight and torment. Maggie and Jenny spent time walking on the beach and talking in front of the fire. Jenny was relieved that Maggie didn't mention her aborted attempt at making love. The thought was so painful that she pushed it out of her mind, but she couldn't keep it out of her dreams. In dreams she felt Maggie's kiss, Maggie's lips against her mouth, Maggie's mouth against her breasts. Her excitement soared as Maggie's hands traced her body and slid gently between her thighs. Pleasure filled her senses, pinning her against her own desire — unwilling to retreat, unable to advance — holding her with her love for Maggie, doing battle against the strength of her past. Her eyes opened to a cold dark room. Darkness was a living thing, assaulting her body and mind, enclosing her in need and fear. Leaving her alone and lonely. Sealing her love inside.

They ate breakfast and walked the beach. In the afternoon they started back to London.

"I'll be out of town until Wednesday evening," Maggie said. She glanced toward Jenny, then back to the road. "I got the assignment in Scotland. The clearance came through Friday. I got word when I checked for messages at the hotel."

Jenny was disappointed. She had been looking forward to time with Maggie and hadn't considered that Maggie would leave London again so soon. "I'll miss you. I was looking forward to your company this week. Now I have no excuse for missing breakfast and lunch with Lillian Reynolds tomorrow."

Maggie flashed a grin in Jenny's direction. "If I could save you I would. I don't know how you put up with the old war horse." She stepped on the brake as the car in front of them slowed and turned off the main road. "The staff isn't supposed to like the chief matron. You actually enjoy the woman."

"I do," Jenny said. She thought of the similarities between Maggie and Lillian Reynolds. Both women were confident in themselves and their work, were ruthless in the name of reaching a goal, and had a definite effect on the people who met them. People liked them immensely, or disliked them with equal intensity. Neither left room for a middle ground. They committed themselves totally to any course they

91

pursued, driven to protect and speak for those less fortunate and more vulnerable than themselves. Jenny smiled. "She reminds me of you."

Maggie raised an eyebrow and threw a quick glance at Jenny. "Please," she said indignantly. "If I ever become as arrogant as her, I hope someone will put me out of my misery."

Amused at Maggie's failure to see their similarities, she said "Take my word for it, you two could be related." She felt warmth and love for Maggie.

"Hmph," Maggie replied. Her eyebrow went up again, and Jenny could see the dimple in her right cheek. "That's not a flattering comparison."

"It is," Jenny said. "You just don't know it."

They made plans to return to Brighton the following weekend.

CHAPTER 15

It was almost 6:45 a.m. when Jenny knocked on Lillian Reynolds' door. The door opened and Jenny was surprised to see Lieutenant Hazel Oaks standing in front of her. Her eyes were red and puffy, as if she'd been crying.

Suddenly Jenny felt she was intruding. "I'm supposed to meet Captain Reynolds for breakfast, but I can see her later if she's busy."

Hazel Oaks looked confused. "I guess you haven't heard; you'd better come in."

"Heard what?" Jenny asked. She was anxious as she walked into Lillian Reynolds' quarters, a combination sitting room and bedroom. Two small cardboard boxes were on the floor in front of a scarred walnut desk. The boxes were filled with papers and books.

"You'd better sit down," Hazel Oaks gestured toward the threadbare floral sofa. It stood against the military plainness of the room like a wild garden at the edge of a desert.

Jenny's heart raced as the beginning of a thought formed in her mind. She closed it out quickly. "Where's Lillian? Is she all right?"

"She was killed Friday night," Hazel Oaks said.

Jenny felt stunned and light-headed. For a moment she thought she was going to be sick. "I just talked to her on Friday afternoon." She sat down heavily on the sofa. "She was planning to visit her sister for the weekend."

Lieutenant Oaks sat down next to Jenny. "That's where it happened. They must have decided not to go to a bomb shelter."

Jenny felt her muscles tighten as the shock ran through her. "Her sister was crippled with arthritis. She couldn't get around very well." Jenny heard her words as if they'd been spoken by someone else.

"The bomb was a direct hit. They were killed instantly," Hazel Oaks said. "We got the word early Saturday morning." She looked at the two small boxes. "Her replacement will be here on Wednesday. I thought I'd pack her things and send them to her brother in Newcastle."

Jenny leaned back and looked around the room. It was empty without Lillian. She felt the warmth of tears on her face. How ironic, to make it through Dunkirk and El Alamein, only to be killed in England. How uncertain life was.

On the end table by the sofa, a small glass paperweight was sitting exactly where she remembered it. She picked it up and looked at the snow-covered scene. Hills and trees looked quiet and peaceful inside the glass bubble. Jenny shook it gently and watched the snow swirl about the tiny world. It looked cold, but inviting. Like the cold days at Brighton. The thought struck like lightning. How easily she could lose Maggie. Her heart beat wildly; her stomach knotted. Fear settled in her chest and inched through her being.

"You look as white as chalk," Hazel said.

Jenny tried to focus her attention on Hazel's words. With great effort she pulled bits and pieces of thoughts together and focused her attention on Hazel. "I'll be fine." She looked at her watch. "I'd better go. I have a class to teach before I make my ward rounds."

It was sheer discipline that allowed Jenny to go on with her classes. She forced her grief and fear into a single corner of her mind and sealed it completely from her public life. She finished her day and retreated into the privacy of her room. Fear hurled itself at her defenses. She shook uncontrollably as her defenses and discipline crumbled. She thought of Lillian, alive and vibrant on Friday afternoon, gone forever on Friday night. No illness to warn of death's approach. No time for acceptance. Nothing to underscore the reality of her loss. An image of Maggie, cold and still, invaded her consciousness. *No!* a voice screamed inside herself. The image faded, then gained new strength. She shook her head. *No, I won't lose her. I can't.* Maggie's smile replaced the mask of death. Jenny felt an urgency to talk to Maggie, to hold her close, to feel her mouth against her lips. Dear God, she thought, please keep her safe. Please bring her back to me.

CHAPTER 16

For the next several days Jenny spent all of her off-duty hours by herself. When classes and office hours were finished, she left the hospital and walked the mile to Saint Stephen's Catholic Church which was often empty in the late afternoon. Jenny sat in the last row on the middle aisle, and for the first ten minutes sank into the silence that surrounded her. She took a deep breath as she acclimated to the large, unpopulated space. Saint Stephen's was one place in London where she could step outside the war, and without interruption, listen to her heart.

97

On the main altar, the sacristy lamp hung from the ceiling to remind visitors that, captured in the Eucharist, imprisoned in the tabernacle, Christ was as present as he had been to his apostles. Jenny had been taught this truth in childhood and had accepted it ever since, without question. Here she could place her feelings upon the altar and hear God's voice within herself.

You know I love her, Jenny prayed. I've tried not to care. Nothing has changed my feelings for her. I no longer fear Your judgment. I'm afraid one of us will be killed before I have the chance to express my love. As quickly as it ended for Lillian.

Jenny felt the finality of death, like a large stone in the pit of her stomach. Please don't let that happen, she prayed. I love her more than I thought it possible to love anyone. I want to build a life with her. I know it won't be easy. That the world will be a constant obstacle to us. But without Maggie, life will be hollow for me. I'm tired of living a lie. I'd rather fight society with Maggie than face life without her. I can't pretend with David anymore. If loving and wanting Maggie is wrong, take the feelings away. But how could love be wrong in a world that knows so little of it? Isn't love a reason to celebrate? Do you really care that the person I love is a woman? Or is it the world alone that condemns us?

She remembered David's words about perversion. I could learn to stand against such things. Not that they wouldn't hurt, but they wouldn't outweigh my love for Maggie. I know she feels the same.

She smiled as she felt the warmth of Maggie's love flow through her. Her eyes focused on the small gold tabernacle. Help me be worthy of the love I feel.

To accept it as a gift. A reflection of Your love. A reflection of Yourself. Be with us when the world isn't. Be for us when friends and family aren't. Accept us when society casts us out. But most of all, witness the love we feel for each other. Bless our longing.

Footsteps echoed behind Jenny. An elderly priest shuffled up the aisle. He stopped and knelt in the first pew. The thought hardened like crystal. Suddenly it didn't matter what the priests taught. They could only pass judgment. And judgment was a poor substitute for love.

CHAPTER 17

The air raid sirens sounded as Jenny increased her pace through the darkened streets. She was still several blocks from the Savoy. In seconds the night was pierced by long fingers of light, frantically searching a moonless sky for enemy planes. The broken rhythm of ack-ack invaded the air as she entered the hotel lobby. She nodded at the desk clerk and went directly to Maggie's room.

"Who is it?" Maggie asked through the closed door.

"It's Jenny. I need to talk to you."

Maggie looked surprised as she opened the door. "What are you doing on the street during an air raid? What's wrong?" She leaned against the edge of her desk.

The V-shaped area of skin visible at the top of Maggie's robe reminded Jenny of the soft firmness of Maggie's breasts, and she felt her stomach muscles contract.

"Lillian Reynolds was killed in an air raid on Friday."

Maggie's face was a mixture of pain and anger. She shook her head. "I'm so sorry, Jenny. I know you cared about her. This damn war has already claimed too many lives."

Jenny felt a resurgence of anxiety. "That's why I'm here, Maggie." She told Maggie what she had gone through since she last saw her.

Maggie's robe gaped slightly, revealing the naked skin of her inner thigh. There was hope in Maggie's face. "Jenny, are you sure about this? Are you really sure?"

Jenny answered with an embrace. Maggie's mouth was warm and sweet as she opened her lips to return Jenny's kiss. The soft curves of Maggie's body pressed against hers.

"I love you, Maggie," Jenny whispered. Her hand moved to the gap in Maggie's robe and caressed her inner thigh. Desire blazed inside her as Maggie's kiss grew more intense.

Maggie pulled her gently toward the bedroom. Logs popped and crackled in the fireplace, and firelight painted everything with a golden glow. She watched their reflection in the mirror as Maggie kissed and caressed her into nakedness. Jenny's mind

101

spun with passion. She pushed the robe from Maggie's shoulders. It fell silently to the floor. She caressed velvet skin and lost herself in another kiss.

"I want you so much," Jenny whispered against Maggie's lips. "I want to please you."

The sheets felt cool against her skin as she lifted her body slightly, anxious to welcome Maggie to herself. Maggie's body was silken firmness. Engulfed with desire, Jenny lay back to accept Maggie's lips, soft and gentle, moving lightly against her forehead, her eyes, her cheek. She parted her lips slowly as Maggie's mouth met hers in a long tender kiss.

Muscles tensed beneath her hands — Maggie's body responding to her touch. Maggie's hands flowed along her body like an incoming tide. Her mouth floated downward, leaving pools of pleasure in its wake. Jenny's nipples stiffened as Maggie drew one, then the other, into her mouth. She moaned and threaded her fingers through Maggie's soft curls.

"Your mouth is so warm," Jenny whispered. "I want to melt and disappear inside you." She caught her breath as Maggie's palm embraced her inner thighs. She cradled Maggie's face in her hands and drew her upward. She welcomed Maggie's tongue and sucked it inside. Maggie's kisses were rougher now, hot and intense, they nibbled at her tongue and lips.

"God, I love you." Maggie spoke against her open mouth and trailed kisses along her neck and shoulders. She shivered as currents of desire followed Maggie's tongue along the hollow of her ribs, along the tautness of her belly, against the longing in her inner thighs. This was pleasure she had never known with David, desire she had never felt for him. She gasped as Maggie's finger entered her, fueling her joy

102

and desire. Ripples of pleasure reached from Maggie's fingertips, growing in intensity as they engulfed her body. She pulled her muscles tight, squeezing Maggie's fingers, holding her fast within her well. Her senses were on fire now, burning Maggie's kisses into her brain. She moaned with delight as Maggie's tongue slid upward, creating new joys with its touch. She trembled as Maggie sucked her inside and ran her tongue against the firmness of the pearl. She surrendered totally to her Lover's song. It exalted her senses, her longing, her love. Maggie's song consumed her, body and soul. She had lost all sense of time and space. She was fire seeking home, light seeking its source, joy seeking its creator.

Maggie's tongue played louder now; it covered lips and pearl, stem and head, with firm insistent strokes. She moaned and closed her eyes as pleasure became unbearable and exploded into a thousand tiny suns. She was part of them now, fire and light, heat and energy, destruction and creation. She pushed her body hard against Maggie's tongue and pulled Maggie's head tighter against the throbbing beat that consumed her.

"Oh . . . Maggie . . . " Her body arched upward and exploded in waves of ecstasy. Never before was love like this . . . It lifted her, surrounded her, consumed her, and created her anew.

"Maggie." Her mouth embraced the name. "Yes, Maggie, yes." She and Maggie were one — one heart, one soul, one love.

Maggie's body covered her as she floated in complete fulfillment. The glow from the fire painted Maggie's face with golden light.

"I love you, Jenny," Maggie whispered. "I'm so glad you're here."

* * * * *

The storm inside had passed. It had raged in her heart and mind, breaking finally against her love for Maggie. The earth and everything in it was new again.

London was still dark as she hurried through the early morning cold toward Saint Elizabeth's. It was five-thirty when she opened the door to her room. She showered quickly and dressed for class. Images of Maggie flowed into her mind. The softness of her mouth had planted its memory deep inside her. Her body trembled as she remembered Maggie's mouth between her thighs.

This won't get me through class or the day, she thought. She checked the seams of her stockings, picked up her notes, and closed the door behind her.

The hospital hallway was hot and stuffy. It smelled of steamed heat and closed windows. Its closeness faded as she recalled the clean scent of Maggie's skin, the taste of her mouth.

She paused outside her classroom and took a deep breath. I love you, Maggie Conover, she thought. I wish you weren't out of town tonight.

CHAPTER 18

Despite Maggie rushing through her assignment and back to London, she and Jenny were two hours late starting for Brighton.

Maggie tried unsuccessfully to keep her mind on her driving. She wanted to look at Jenny, and her body ached for Jenny's touch. Jenny's hand nestled on her leg as she drove. Maggie tried half-heartedly to discuss her assignment and Jenny's class, but she was besieged and overwhelmed with thoughts and feelings. She noticed Jenny's speech too was rapid and her tone higher than normal.

She doesn't want to tell me about class any more than I want to tell her about my assignment, Maggie thought. She glanced at Jenny. Her brown eyes were riveted on Maggie and looked out of sync with her words. They were intense and filled with a questioning sensuality.

"I can't stand this." Maggie checked the deserted road ahead and the empty highway behind them. Not a car in sight!

"What's wrong?" Jenny said, evidently concerned.

Maggie pulled the car to the shoulder of the road and cut the engine. Without a word she turned toward Jenny and took her into her arms. Jenny's mouth welcomed her kiss. Lips parted easily to admit Maggie within. Maggie slipped her hand inside Jenny's coat and cupped the firm, large breast. She could hear Jenny's breathing quicken, matching her own shallow breaths as their kiss grew more intense.

Jenny brushed her open mouth against Maggie's lips. "Unless you plan to make love right here we'd better get back on the road," Jenny said.

Maggie kissed her again, unwilling to release her, pressing her tongue deep inside Jenny's mouth. "God, I want to make love to you." Maggie's voice was a hoarse whisper.

Jenny bit Maggie's tongue lightly, playfully, and then said, "I'm not kidding." Her eyes, reflecting moonlight, were glazed with desire. "Either make love to me here or start driving."

Maggie's hands were trembling as she separated herself from Jenny. "I hope we make it to Brighton before I melt."

* * * * *

106

Naked, they lay in Maggie's bed caressing each other's breasts and watching as erect nipples became rigid beneath their fingers. Maggie's body contoured Jenny's perfectly — curves fit together like a puzzle. She brushed Jenny's nipples with her own as Jenny's hands moved along her stomach. Maggie's muscles quivered in response. Jenny's tongue played along her lips and cheeks and sent its fire deep inside her mouth.

Maggie inched downward, nibbling Jenny's breasts. She could hear faint murmuring from Jenny's throat. It grew in intensity as Maggie continued her descent. The silk of Jenny's thighs was soft against her mouth. It glided like water beneath her searching tongue.

The scent of musk filled her senses. Her tongue tasted the sweet and salt of Jenny's love. She opened her mouth and took it to herself. Soft, pliant folds caressed her mouth like the silky petals of a flower. Her fingers stroked the hidden well — delighting in its wet warmth. The flower expanded as she sucked its sweetness, opening gently as her tongue explored the separate petals and made its way to the flower's heart. Jenny was moving slowly now, undulating against her mouth. She pushed the tiny bud hard against Maggie's teeth, rubbing its tender heart around and around until passion flowed in Maggie's blood, consuming her. She was abandon with one desire: to drive Jenny trembling into orgasmic pleasure. Jenny's fingers kneaded Maggie's hair, urging her attention to the center of Jenny's desire. Her murmuring became a low moaning sound as Maggie's tongue covered the pearl completely, holding it firmly, stroking it wildly, strumming its engorged head with every burning stroke.

Maggie felt the passion between her thighs burst into flame. Her cry was a deep moaning sound, held tight against the flower, lifting Jenny and herself into ecstasy.

Her body curled with pleasure as she pushed herself harder against the flower's face. Jenny's scream pierced the night. Jenny pulled her upward and kissed her. Their tongues glided in the wetness of their love, drinking in its taste and fragrance.

She didn't wait for Maggie to respond. Jenny's hand burrowed between Maggie's thighs to the satiny wetness. Separating and stroking, Jenny's touch was tentative at first, but grew in confidence as Maggie responded. Maggie groaned as her pleasure began its climb. She pulled Jenny to her and buried herself in Jenny's kiss.

Maggie's nipples were on Jenny's lips. She sucked them in, holding their firmness against the rhythm of her tongue as Maggie's hips danced faster now, her hands guiding Jenny's head gently downward. The message fueled Jenny's desire, and she longed to feel Maggie inside her mouth, to fill Maggie with the pleasure she had known. She shivered with delight as she tasted Maggie for the first time and stroked the silken folds. The pearl was firm and erect, a separate point for love's ministry, as she sucked it inward, massaging it consonantly with her tongue and lips. Excitement shot through her as Maggie moaned with pleasure and pushed herself against Jenny's lips and teeth. Her body shuddered with ecstasy as she pushed Jenny's mouth away and drew her upward.

Maggie's body was hot and wet against her own. She quivered in response as Maggie's mouth covered hers completely and Maggie's tongue plunged deep within her.

Her words were breathless at first, growing in strength as she spoke. "I love you so much." Her arms tightened around Jenny. "I want to take you inside me. To lose myself in you." She kissed her forehead, then her lips. "I never dreamed it could be this perfect."

"I've never loved anyone as much," Jenny said. "I don't want to stop touching you."

"You don't have to stop," Maggie said. "Just give me five minutes to catch my breath." She enfolded Jenny in her arms. "Just lie next to me for a while. We have all weekend to make love." The music of Harry James filled the room with softness.

They slept in each other's arms, waking several times, making love, drifting again into sleep.

* * * * *

Day replaced night. A shaft of gray light entered the window and fell across the bed. Jenny propped her head against her palm and looked at Maggie's face, peaceful and childlike in sleep. She could feel the pressure of Maggie's leg as it rested on hers. The sound of Maggie's breathing was quiet and rhythmic. It had a soothing effect on Jenny, enhancing the warm contentment of the morning. She ran her hand through Maggie's blonde curls. They moved through her fingers like liquid gold.

How beautiful you are, she thought. How passionate and tender. I never dreamed I could want somebody so much. She brushed her fingertips against Maggie's cheek and traced the outline of her eyes. Maggie's mouth was full and inviting. Excitement rushed through Jenny as she remembered last night's fire, its memory lingering on her skin, warming her even now. She leaned forward and kissed Maggie's lips where the taste of love still clung.

Jenny moved her body closer. I love you, Maggie, she thought.

Maggie's eyelids fluttered and closed again. She moved against Jenny's body and slid her hand between Jenny's thighs. Her fingers moved in long light strokes. Maggie's mouth met hers in a long, slow kiss.

Jenny gasped as Maggie entered her. Her fingers plunged deep, then shallow, then deeper again. They stroked the upper wall as they danced to passion's tune. Maggie's free hand pressed downward over Jenny's pubic bone, her thumb massaged the excited pearl, stroking it to a new firmness. Her fingers danced faster as she pushed harder against Jenny's throbbing center. Jenny's hips matched Maggie's rhythm and force perfectly. She gasped, then shuddered, as pleasure exploded inside her, sending long lines of fiery energy throughout her body. "Oh, Maggie." Her voice was barely a whisper. She wrapped her arms around Maggie and pulled her firmly against herself. Her body shook as waves of ecstasy washed over her. She fell against Maggie, spent and satisfied.

"Good morning," Maggie said. "What a nice way to start the day."

It was Sunday afternoon before they dressed and left the cottage.

CHAPTER 19

Jenny was particularly homesick as Christmas approached. She and Maggie had spent a long Thanksgiving weekend at Brighton, and since Thanksgiving is not a holiday in Great Britain, Jenny was able to obtain the extended pass. She was expected to return the courtesy at Christmas. Jenny would work on the wards during the week before Christmas, and would begin a one-week furlough on December 26th. She and Maggie would spend the time at Brighton.

Having worked the 11 p.m. to 7 a.m. shift on Christmas day, she arrived at Maggie's suite tired.

"It was one of those nights when everything goes wrong," Jenny said. She hugged Maggie and kissed her again. "I could use some coffee." She looked at the fireplace. "The fire smells great."

Maggie turned her toward the bathroom and slapped her playfully on the backside. "You get a shower and I'll call room service for coffee and toast. It should be here by the time you get out."

The warm shower revived her. She wrapped herself in her bathrobe, towel-dried her hair, and walked into the bedroom. Maggie was under the covers, sitting up against a pillow. She was naked from the waist up.

Jenny sat on the bed, leaned forward, and kissed her breast. "What happened to your pajamas?" She ran her hand over Maggie's nipples.

"The same thing that's about to happen to your robe." She reached for the sash around Jenny's waist and unfastened the tie.

There was a knock on the door.

"Damn," Maggie said. "I forgot about our coffee."

"Maybe they'll go away. Ignore it."

"If we do we can forget room service for the rest of the war." Maggie started to get up.

"Stay there," Jenny said. "I'll get it."

Jenny opened the door and froze. "David," she said. "What are you doing here?"

David paled then reddened, anger rising in his blue eyes. He looked down the length of her robe and back to her face. Jenny was terrified.

Without a word David pushed the door back and walked past Jenny toward the bedroom.

"David, wait a minute," Jenny called after him. She grabbed his arm, but he yanked away.

He stood two steps into the room and stared at the bed. Maggie had pulled the covers over her breasts. Jenny stepped in front of him. "Let's talk in the other room," she said, her heart racing.

"You goddamned bitch," David snarled.

Before Jenny realized what was happening, she felt a sharp pain against her left cheek and was falling to the floor.

"I ought to kill you." David's voice was filled with rage.

Jenny's ear was ringing. She looked up and saw Maggie standing to David's right. She had put on a robe and she was holding a poker.

"Don't hit her again," Maggie said. Her voice sounded as if it was far away.

David's face was twisted into a horrible snarl. He sneered at Maggie. "You'd kill for her, would you? How touching. Neither of you is worth killing." He nodded at Jenny. "Get dressed. You're leaving."

"The hell she is," Maggie said. "Get the hell out of here before I call the police." Her eyes narrowed with determination.

"Really? I'll bet they'd love to hear about you two." He glanced at Jenny. "If I leave without you, I'll be back with the military police."

Jenny knew David meant what he said. She stood up, dizzy, her ear still ringing. "Wait in the lobby. I'll get dressed and meet you in fifteen minutes."

"No," Maggie said. "You don't have to leave with him. Let him get the police. There's no law against you being here."

113

David closed his hands into fists. "You bitch. Do you think you can fuck my wife and get off scot free?" He took a half step toward Maggie. "You'll pay for this. No one takes what belongs to me. I'll have you thrown out of England. We don't like queers here. You won't be the first one who's gone to jail." He turned to Jenny. "If you're not downstairs in ten minutes, your girlfriend can say good-bye to her newspaper career." He left and slammed the door behind him.

Jenny sat on the side of the bed and held her head in her hands. "I can't believe this," she said.

Maggie dropped the poker, knelt in front of her and lifted her face. "Jenny, please don't go with him." There was desperation in her voice. "He's already hit you. He can't prove a thing. It's his word against ours. He can't prove we weren't dressed." Her tone was imperative. "Stay here. We'll face him together."

Jenny began to dress. "I can't, Maggie. He'll do what he says. He'll ruin you if I don't go with him." She looked into Maggie's eyes. "He'll also see to it that I get a dishonorable discharge. I don't want that to happen. Not to either of us."

"He's bluffing. He wouldn't do that to you."

"You don't know him, Maggie. He'd do anything for revenge." She wrapped her arms around Maggie. "Maybe I can talk some sense into him. I have to try." She walked toward the door. "I'd better hurry. He'll leave if I'm not down there on time."

Maggie held Jenny by the shoulders. "Where will you be? When will I hear from you?"

"I don't know," Jenny said. She recognized the panic in Maggie's eyes. "I have to be on duty on Monday morning. I'll call you right after work." She pulled Maggie to herself. "I love you, Maggie. I don't want you hurt."

CHAPTER 20

David led Jenny to a small hotel three blocks from the Savoy. He was seething. The image of Jenny naked beneath her bathrobe, of Maggie naked in bed, stoked the fires inside him. He paced the room trying to gain control before he spoke. Jenny was seated in a wingback chair opposite the foot of the bed. He stopped and looked at her. Her face was pale, her eyes direct.

She's not afraid of me, he thought. She will be.

He pulled an identical chair directly in front of Jenny. It made a scraping noise on the hardwood floor and bumped onto the rug. He sat down and leaned toward her, remembering the interrogation techniques he had been taught for German prisoners and willing himself into that role. She'll be a lot more respectful when I'm finished with her, he thought.

"Do you have any idea of the position you've put me in?" He didn't wait for an answer. "I'll be the laughing-stock of my ship if this gets around." The thought fueled more anger.

"No one else knows, David," Jenny said sarcastically. "Your reputation is safe."

"Is it?" He found her attitude irritating. "For your sake, I hope you're right. Because if you're not, I'll make sure that you and that bitch never forget how I feel about it."

"We've been discreet." Her eyes still looked at him directly. Her apparent lack of guilt or shame infuriated him.

"Were you now? What you're saying is you're a good sneak." He could feel the heat rising in his face. "Why the hell did you do such a thing? It couldn't be for sex. You're not what I'd call a passionate girl. You never seemed to enjoy the little sex we had." He waited for his words to sink in. The important thing now was to keep this quiet. "Do you know why you did it? Did she rape you? We can have her arrested and thrown out of England. Just say the word. It will help me know you want to put our marriage back together."

Jenny's face was fluid. Emotions played over it in rapid succession. Anger, disbelief, contempt, determination. She looked directly at him. "Maggie didn't do anything I didn't want her to do."

117

His rage was uncontrollable. Where was her shame? Her guilt?

"Do you know what you're saying? That you actually wanted her hands on you?" David resisted the temptation to slap her. To knock her to the floor. "Have you gone mad? Would you really give up your marriage for a relationship with that . . ." His anger caught in his throat. ". . . that *thing?*"

"We haven't had much of a marriage. What we've had is you telling me how to live my life," Jenny said, coldly.

"That's what marriage is," David said. "What it's supposed to be. A husband building a life for himself and his family. I'm the head of our house. I make the decisions."

"Not for me you don't. Not anymore." Jenny's face was crimson.

He knew she was close to exploding. In a way, he'd welcome that. They could meet head on and have it out once and for all. Once he had made his superiority clear to her, once she understood that she had no choice, they could be finished with this power struggle.

"Really? Who does? That abomination you've taken for a lover?" He clenched his fists. "I could kill you for what you've done. You're nothing but a slut. When I think how considerate I was with you about sex . . . How I never asked you for things that weren't considered a lady's place." He grabbed Jenny's wrist and held it tight.

She pulled her arm and he tightened his hold. "You're hurting me," Jenny said.

"I'm going to do a lot more than that to you." He moved his face within inches of Jenny. "You're

118

going to do anything I want. And believe me, there's a lot I haven't asked." He twisted her wrist, wanting to hurt her. "But if you can go to bed with another girl, you can sure see that your husband has what he wants."

"You'll have to kill me first. I haven't the slightest intention of ever sleeping with you again. I want a divorce," Jenny hissed.

"Well, you're not getting one," he said. He pushed Jenny's wrist away roughly and moved his face close to Jenny's. "I've always wanted to know what it would take to excite you. I intend to find out, and you'll cooperate or pay the consequences."

"You disgust me," Jenny said. "Divorce or no divorce, I'm leaving you."

He pulled himself to his full six foot three inches and looked down at her. "Not unless you want yourself and your girlfriend turned over to the military intelligence. I'll make sure she never works for another newspaper." He hated her now. "And I'll see to it that you receive a dishonorable discharge. You'll never get another job as a nurse."

"You'd destroy two lives just because you didn't get what you wanted?"

He was encouraged by the fear he saw in her face. "In the blink of an eye," he said. "If you don't believe it, try me."

"Why would you hold me like that? I don't want to be with you." Jenny's voice was on the edge of hysteria. "I don't want you touching me."

"That's unfortunate," David said. He felt exhilarated by his new-found power over Jenny. "You'll cooperate, or I go to military intelligence."

* * * * *

The following hour was hell for Jenny. She was completely humiliated by the things David had said and done to her.

"I can't stand this," Jenny cried as she pushed David away from her. She pulled the sheet over her naked body and fought back her tears. She was horrified as David's face became a gruesome sneer.

"It's your choice," he said. "Either you put out for me, or I'll put your girlfriend out of business for good. She won't be able to get a job selling papers, let alone writing for them." He glared at her, hate burning in his eyes. "You should also give some thought to how your parents will react when they learn their daughter is a queer. Believe me, if I have to, I'll tell them the whole story."

Jenny felt defeated. There was nothing she could do without destroying the people she cared most about. She let go of the sheet as David pulled it from her body. He pressed his mouth over hers with such force that her lip split against her teeth. With the taste of iron in her mouth, she closed her eyes and escaped into Maggie's arms.

120

CHAPTER 21

After one week with no word from Jenny, Maggie was crazy with pain and worry. She weighed the pros and cons of contacting Jenny and finally gave in to her feelings and went to Jenny's office.

"I'm sorry if I'm disturbing you." Maggie took the chair in front of Jenny's desk. "I have to talk to you."

Jenny looked tired. Her eyes were red and underscored with dark circles.

"Why didn't you call me, Jenny? You must have known how worried I'd be."

"I started to call several days ago," Jenny said, her voice flat, not at all like herself. "I didn't want to face the truth. And I didn't want to share the truth with you."

Maggie was frightened. Whatever the truth is, she thought, it's going to hurt. She thought about leaving Jenny's office before it was too late. Before the truth was out and couldn't be unheard.

"I'm back with David," Jenny said. "I won't be getting a divorce."

Maggie felt as if a strong fist had punched her in the stomach. This can't be true, she thought. I must have misunderstood. She closed her eyes for a second and took a deep breath. Oh God, let it not be true. She wanted to ask why but had lost control of her voice. She could only stare at Jenny in hurt and disbelief.

"This isn't what I want, Maggie," Jenny said. She walked around the desk and leaned against it. "I asked David for a divorce. He won't give me one."

Maggie felt new hope. If that was the only problem, they could work it out. "Leave him," she said. "He'll come around in time."

"I can't, Maggie. He'll ruin us if I continue seeing you. If I leave he'll go to Military Intelligence. He'll make sure that we're both expelled from England." She told Maggie about David's threats. "He means it, Maggie. He's insane with hate and revenge." A tear rolled slowly down her cheek. "I couldn't stand it if I was the cause of you losing everything. I just couldn't live with that."

Maggie wanted to take Jenny into her arms but she resisted, remembering there was no lock on Jenny's office door. "My God, Jenny, if I lose you there's nothing left. I don't care what David does to me. I can find other work."

"You love your work. You wouldn't be happy in anything else," Jenny said.

"Not as much as I love you." Maggie had never pleaded like this before. Not with another human being. Not ever.

"It wouldn't work, Maggie. David wouldn't let it. He's threatened to turn me in to the military. That would mean a dishonorable discharge. I'd never get another job in nursing."

"You could do something else. We could go away together." Panic took possession of her. "You have to give us a chance."

Jenny knelt and enclosed Maggie's hands between her own. Her eyes pleaded for understanding. "Listen to what you're saying, Maggie." Jenny's voice was as soft as velvet. "It won't work. You know that." Tears fell on Maggie's hands — Jenny's tears. "It would be hard enough to face society. I could risk that. But I can't face life if you're destroyed. You'd end up hating me."

Jenny's eyes broke contact for a second, then returned to Maggie's face. She took a deep breath. "And I couldn't face my life if I'm thrown out of the Army. I don't want to find another job. I love nursing."

Maggie stumbled beneath the weight of Jenny's words. "I thought you loved me."

"I do love you. More than anyone in this world. But I won't destroy you with my love. If I did, there'd be nothing left for me — nothing left for us."

Maggie felt drawn to Jenny's eyes — eyes she had entered in the past, tumbling gladly into their depths.

She pulled her glance away and flung her feelings against the cold wall of thought, barring their escape with rock hard logic. My love could destroy her. There's no way to win. She dug her nails into her palms and hoped the pain would keep her together, at least until she was alone.

Jenny was speaking again. Maggie gathered her attention and focused it on her words. "I don't want you to lose everything for me. I couldn't ask that of you. And I couldn't accept it as a gift."

Maggie felt the warm wetness of tears begin to flow down her face.

"Please, Maggie, don't make me say any more. Just wish me well and let me live my life in peace."

The words tore at Maggie's heart like jagged claws, tearing and shredding tender flesh, wounding her love almost to the death.

Jenny squeezed Maggie's hands. "Please don't make me hurt you more than I have."

Maggie was conscious of the separation of her hands from Jenny's as she stood up, aware of the separation of their hearts. She pulled herself erect, as if a rod had been placed against her spine. Without another word she walked out the door and pulled it closed behind her.

Reality sent its icy fingers into her heart and mind. It filled her with loneliness and longing. How can I live without you Jenny? How can I survive without your love?

CHAPTER 22

In the weeks following her breakup with Maggie, Jenny experienced a kind of depression and emotional pain unlike any she had ever felt before. Her thoughts were filled with Maggie — Maggie's face, Maggie's voice, Maggie's touch. Memories of their love intruded into her days, and came alive each night in her dreams. It took all the concentration Jenny could gather to complete her assignments as if nothing in her world had changed. In truth, her life had been turned upside down. Her anger at David had fermented into rage, a rage that grew stronger every day. David's deliberate abuse had hurt and humiliated her beyond all power of forgiveness. She was trapped by a man who had violated her physically and emotionally. He had made it too dangerous to have what she wanted most. He had turned her love for Maggie into a weapon — a weapon that could kill them both. For this, and for every day she spent without Maggie in her life, she hated the man she no longer considered her husband. She was convinced that nothing could quiet the rage she felt, or remove it from the forefront of her mind.

* * * * *

The word came so quickly she didn't have time to consider the change it meant in her life. Within minutes of receiving their orders, Jenny's company was sealed off from the outside world, trucked to a nearby port, and placed aboard ships. They would be the medical support for a new allied invasion.

Jenny stood in the hatchway of the small cabin and allowed the sight of it to sink into her mind. How dismal, she thought as her eyes moved over the cold gray bulkheads and metal double decker bunks. Of all the places to get locked up in, this has to be the worst. Who but the Army could put a claustrophobic in an inside cabin? She felt beads of perspiration take shape on her forehead and upper lip and fought the panic that was bobbing around inside her. She'd have to handle this fear, just as she'd have to handle her fear of being in a combat situation. It was her duty, and as difficult as it might be, she would keep her commitment.

She sat on the edge of her bunk and listened. The constant hum of the ship's huge engines settled into the background, a canvas against which all other sounds defined themselves. The two British and one American nurses who shared the tiny cabin were involved in conversation about possible landing sites. Jenny found their topic less than comforting. She shifted her attention to the narrow passageway that ran the length of the deck. She could hear the muffled voices of nurses as they made their way from cabin to cabin locating friends for future visits. An occasional male voice stood out as a crew member or physician walked along the passageway.

Jenny's heart lurched as the heavy steel hatch swung open and clanked against the bulkhead. She saw Alice Martin, a long beanpole of a nurse, standing one step into the cabin. "The mess hall will open in ten minutes," she said. "Might as well eat while we can. Who knows how long we'll have calm seas."

* * * * *

Jenny lay awake in the stuffy darkness. She could hear the rhythmic breathing of her cabin mates and the moaning of the ship as it rocked gently through the night.

Images of Maggie slid into her mind as easily as day follows night. She could feel Maggie's body pressing against her own, her skin warm and smooth, with a clean fresh scent that enticed her senses and increased her need for closeness. Desire grew in her, rising from below, reaching upward, enfolding her in its heat. Desire became a physical pain. It closed

127

tightly inside her, adding its strength to the loneliness she felt. She wanted Maggie more than she believed possible. More than Maggie's physical touch, she wanted Maggie's emotional presence and the union of mind and body their love produced. The need became unbearable. She could no longer endure the longing.

The deck was cold against her bare feet as she searched in the darkness for her shoes.

She got up and dressed as quietly as possible. The woolen slacks and shirt felt rough against her skin. Carrying her shoes, she walked noiselessly to the hatch and opened it just far enough to slip into the passageway.

The night was sprinkled with stars. The smell of salt air was clean and alive. How beautiful, she thought, as she walked to the ship rail and looked out over the sea. Black satin waves rose and fell as they rushed toward the ship. They rocked it gently, a baby asleep in their arms. A full moon hung above the horizon and spread its silver light against the blackness of the night.

She pushed her hands into the warm pockets of her field jacket and strolled along the deck. For a moment she gave her attention to the dark silhouettes of ships in the convoy. She focused on what she knew was the HMHS Newfoundland. Like her own ship, HMHS Dorsetshire, it was a floating hospital, complete with operating theaters, X-ray department, and dispensary. Many of the inner bulkheads had been removed, creating large wards that could comfortably hold five hundred patients. Like all hospital ships under the Geneva Convention, it was painted white, with a wide green band down each side, and large red crosses plainly in sight. The ships sailed completely lighted at night — gigantic white elephants, sitting ducks for unscrupulous German pilots. There were no running lights tonight, nor would there be when sailing without patients and on their way to a hopefully unexpected invasion.

What great targets we make, Jenny thought.

"Shouldn't you be asleep?" A woman's whisper startled her. She turned and saw Rebecca Willis standing at her side.

"I wish I could sleep," Jenny said. She kept her voice low, remembering how easily sound carried over water. "What are you doing up here?"

"Looking for you. I thought you might need some company." Rebecca's voice was warm and caring. "It might help to talk."

"Not unless it can give me a large dose of courage," Jenny responded. "I'm not sure I should be here at all."

Rebecca put her hand on Jenny's arm. "We're all scared, Jenny. I had the same doubts when I was on my way to North Africa. I'm scared now. But I know when the time comes I'll do my job. So will you."

"I hope you're right. But nobody on this ship looks as scared as I feel."

"Believe me, they're just as terrified as you are. Some people just hide it better. You have to know where to look. People can keep fear out of their voice, out of their conversations, but they can't keep it out of their eyes. Look in their eyes, Jenny. You'll see that they're all just as frightened as you are. Anyone with good sense will feel afraid at the thought of people shooting at them. There's no such thing as a safe casualty clearing station."

Jenny smiled. "Somehow I don't find that comforting. I thought women were supposed to be kept safe behind the lines."

"I hate to be the one to take away your innocence, but nurses have always been in combat situations. They've served on hospital ships and died trying to save patients when the ships were bombed. They've served on every beachhead of this war. They don't actually go in with the first assault troops but it's only a matter of hours or at the most a few days before we're on the beach. When the troops move up, we move up."

Rebecca Willis put her hand on Jenny's shoulder. "British Sisters have won the George medal, and American nurses have won the Silver Star. Those medals aren't given lightly. You and I belong to a proud tradition. We come from a long line of volunteers who go where they're needed most, and protect their patients with their lives if necessary."

"That sounds like a lot to live up to," Jenny said. "I hope I can do it."

"You'll do fine," Rebecca Willis declared.

CHAPTER 23

The attacks on the convoy had begun during their third day at sea. The daylight raids continued with only an hour or two of reprieve between bomber waves.

Jenny lay in her bunk listening to the planes, bombs, and anti-aircraft guns. The ship vibrated with the shock waves of bursting shells and exploding bombs.

On the first day of the attack Jenny and several nurses watched the approaching planes from a gangway on the upper deck. When two planes scored direct hits with their cannons, shells slamming into the outer bulkhead and across the forward deck, no one had to ask them to go below. Jenny remained below during each successive attack. Flat on her back, or facing the inside bulkhead, she tried to read. It took immense determination to focus her mind on something other than the war and death.

A bomb exploded close to the Dorsetshire. The concussion rocked the ship and sent loose objects — hair brushes, photographs, and books, flying across the cabin. Jenny dropped the book she was trying to read and grabbed the sides of her bunk to avoid being tossed onto the deck. A knot of fear tightened in her stomach and cold perspiration covered her forehead and upper lip. As she picked up her book she realized that her hands were shaking violently. She put the book down and turned to face the inside bulkhead. Her entire body was trembling. Her mouth and throat were bone dry and her heart was pounding against her chest. She tried to gather enough saliva so she could swallow but her efforts were in vain.

Suddenly, as abruptly as it had begun, it was over. The ship's guns fired for several minutes, but there were no incoming shells, planes, or bombs. Jenny closed her eyes and took a deep breath. How awful war is, she thought. How utterly terrifying. No wonder the men are afraid. Anyone with half a mind would be scared. She thought of Maggie and her body began to relax.

* * * * *

Her stomach muscles ached as she leaned over her bunk and wretched into an emesis. Nothing. She had emptied her stomach yesterday, only hours after the storm hit. She had forced herself to take liquids, but even water wouldn't stay down. A doctor and the chief matron had visited the cabin that morning. They injected an anti-emetic and instructed everyone to drink as much liquid as they could manage. Before leaving they had assured all four nurses that they were not unique in experiencing sea sickness. As if to prove his statement, the doctor suddenly grabbed Rebecca's emesis basin and heaved into it. Dry. Jenny could see the lines of perspiration across his forehead. His coloring was an unhealthy gray. He returned the basin and moved toward the hatch. The Dorsetshire pitched left, tossing him and the matron against the bulkhead. "I'll be back this evening," the doctor gasped. "Stay as still as possible."

The storm and the nausea continued to the landing site. An hour before the first assault wave was to go ashore, the storm relented. Jenny studied Doctor Beal's face as he gave her another injection. He looked tired and slightly green. "It's not a secret anymore," he said. "We're landing at Anzio-Nutino. It's an Italian resort city. Our first assault hit the beach at two-thirty a.m." He patted Jenny's arm. "Glad to be on solid land is my guess." He put a fresh cup of water by Jenny's bunk. "We'll be going in ourselves in a couple of days."

"I'd be happy to volunteer to go today," Rebecca Willis said. "If I can just stand on something that doesn't rock, I won't even complain about getting shot at."

133

* * * * *

By the time she climbed over the side of the ship
and scrambled down the net into the landing craft,
Jenny's seasickness had subsided to an almost
tolerable level. She was thankful she was not one of
the nurses left on board due to severe seasickness.
Mal de mer had exacted an awesome toll from the
convoy. Several hundred men and fifteen nurses were
too sick to stand, let alone participate in an
amphibious assault.

The landing craft was packed with nurses and the
necessary equipment to establish Casualty Clearing
Station Number 14 on the beach. Twenty-four nurses
and six physicians rode in with the bandages,
medicines, and surgical instruments. They looked
exhausted. The ship's guns and artillery fire from the
Germans had made sleeping during the three days
almost impossible.

She glimpsed at Rebecca Willis for a second, and
recognized the look of fear on her face. Their eyes
met for an instant, conveying a sense of comraderie
and understanding.

Jenny lost her footing as the LST ran up on the
beach and stopped. There was the shrill sound of
metal scraping on metal as the tailgate opened and
landed with a loud thud on the wet beach. Jenny
drew back as people ahead of her started to move.
This is it, she thought. No more wondering. She
recognized Rebecca Willis' voice: "Kincade, you're
with me. Stay close."

Her first steps on land were anything but dry.
She stepped off the LST and sank into ankle-deep
mud. Her shoes made a sharp sucking sound as she

pulled them free and slogged her way up the beach. She felt detached, as if she was trapped in a frightening unreality.

"Couldn't they find a beach with sand?" a woman's voice called from behind her.

"At least it's not rocking," another called back.

Jenny looked up the beach. It was crowded with troops and equipment. She could see the ruins of bombed out buildings huddled in a straight line three hundred yards from the water's edge. In the distance to her left, jeeps and crates were stockpiled in neat rows. She could barely make out the words REPLACEMENT PARTS on many of the crates.

"Number 14," a man's voice called. "Over here."

Jenny followed automatically as her unit veered to the right. They passed CCS #3 which was already accepting its first casualties. Stretchers were lined up in uneven rows in front and on both sides of the mud-splattered tents.

A nurse looked up from her patient. "Step lively, girls," she called. Her face was covered with blood and mud. "We've been expecting you."

A loud roaring drowned out the woman's voice.

"Eighty-eights," a man shouted. The roar stopped with a loud explosion. A German shell fell a hundred yards from the beach. Jenny froze in terror.

"Get down," a woman shouted. Jenny felt herself falling as the woman threw herself against her legs. The left side of her face slapped against the mud as a loud roaring sound passed overhead.

Jenny looked up and saw Rebecca Willis glaring at her. "This isn't a walk in the park, Jenny. When you hear that roar, hit the dirt."

"That thing sounds like a train. What the hell are they shooting at us?" Jenny took Rebecca's hand and pulled herself up. Her uniform was covered with mud.

"Eighty-eights," Rebecca Willis said. "They're firing anti-aircraft guns at us. The bastards."

A young American soldier straightened Jenny's backpack. "The Captain is right, Ma'am. The Gerries have batteries of the damn things in the hills overlooking the beach."

The soldier led them up the beach and disappeared into the group that was putting tents up for surgeries, X-ray, and hospital wards.

In two hours CCS #14 was open and receiving casualties. They came by ambulance, jeep, stretcher, and on foot. They piled up quickly around the receiving station.

"Tell number three they can close," the Chief Matron called to the radio operator. "We're open for business."

The practice of alternating the receiving of casualties between the variously numbered Casualty Clearing Stations had been designed to provide a breather for an overworked and exhausted medical staff. One CCS would accept wounded for twelve hours, then close, routing the new casualties to the next CCS. The "closed" station then had time to treat and process its wounded, evacuating them to England and elsewhere, making room for the next wave of wounded men.

Jenny was assigned to triage. She would see the wounded first, classify their wounds by severity, and send them to the appropriate treatment tent in a priority order. The wounded who were in no danger of losing their lives waited while physicians and nurses worked to save the more seriously injured.

She stood on the edge of a patchwork quilt of wounded bodies. They lay on narrow canvas stretchers along the ground before her. There were hundreds of them, each torn, ripped, or broken. She stood motionless, her senses overwhelmed by the obscenity before her eyes. Cries of pain and bargaining prayers rose from the frightened men before her and buried themselves in her mind. Their anguish cut through the noise of planes, guns and bombs — more powerful in their effects upon her heart.

"We're ready, Sister." A young corpsman touched Jenny on the arm. "We can start in the left corner and work our way through to the upper right."

His words and touch brought her back to her reason for being there. She rubbed her eyes and refocused on the wounded.

"Right. Let's get started."

She wove her way through the maze of bleeding bodies. Little by little her feelings became numb; it was a merciful and enabling sleep. She moved quickly, dispatching patients to surgery, X-ray, or medical treatment tents. For some, it was already too late. They were carried to a make-shift morgue.

"Sucking chest wound here. Surgery. Stat," she said without looking up. She tied a red tag to the man's ankle. "You'll be fine," she said, and patted the soldier's shoulder. His eyes revealed his terror. Their fear stayed with her as one of the stretcher teams hurried him off to the surgeons.

Four hours later there was a lull in the flow of wounded men. Jenny sat on a muddy underblock that had helped keep the stretchers from sinking into the mud. Her back ached from leaning over the wounded and the dead. Her neck was stiff and she slowly rotated her head hoping to work out some of the pain. She took a deep breath and relaxed her shoulders. She thought: I don't think I've ever been so tired.

There was a loud explosion up the beach, then a roaring sound overhead.

They're at it again, she thought. Don't they ever take a break? Explosions went off in a random pattern. She marveled that the entire beachhead wasn't blown out of existence. Everything and everybody was so tightly packed into the long narrow area that it seemed impossible for anyone to shoot in their direction and not hit something.

At 2000 hours Jenny and the rest of her shift was relieved for the night. They would return to duty eleven hours later, at 0700.

She shared her tent with two other nurses. One was on nights so there would only be two women billeted in the tent at any one time. She was happy that Rebecca shared her tent and her timetable.

Jenny sat on a small canvas cot and looked around the tent. The Tommies had done an excellent job of digging the Sisters in — one of the benefits of being assigned to an allied unit that was mainly British, she thought. After all, American nurses had to dig in and set up their own tents.

She looked around slowly. The area under her tent had been dug into the ground to a depth of five feet. The mud-slick sides had been shored up with timber carried across the ocean on the troop ships. Two large planks ran across the mud floor, one crossing the other at midpoint. They allowed women to move about without sinking into the soft gray ooze that comprised the foundation of the beachhead.

She heard someone walking down the wooden steps that led to her area. She looked toward the sound and was delighted to see Rebecca Willis step into the soft yellow light of the kerosene lamp.

"How's it going?" Rebecca asked. She sat down heavily on the canvas cot across from Jenny. "You look tired, but I don't see any blood on you. Not your own anyway."

Jenny saw a warm smile beneath Rebecca's mud-caked face. "Not yet," Jenny said. "The way those eighty-eights come in, it could be just a matter of time."

Rebecca stretched out on her cot and looked at Jenny. "Everything is just a matter of time. I'm too tired to take my boots off."

A roaring approached from the north, overhead, passed them and continued toward the convoy. Another shell followed close behind.

Jenny was afraid as she looked up, her heartbeat quickening. The top of the tent had a narrow, center opening where a thin slice of black sky shone through. "Don't they ever run out of those damn things? They sound like boxcars coming in sideways."

"After awhile you won't even notice them," Rebecca said with a sigh.

* * * * *

The days became more hectic. The only time Jenny was unaware of her fear was when she was

139

working with patients. But even then, fear occasionally surfaced.

Maggie filled her thoughts every day and dominated her dreams at night. The thought of Maggie's smile could calm her worst fears. At night her body remembered Maggie's hands upon her skin, Maggie's mouth warm and hungry for her kiss.

The horrors she saw proved to her the fleeting nature of life. When this is finally over, she thought, I'll find Maggie and tell her how I feel. If she still wants me, in spite of David's threats, we'll face him and the world together. I'd rather do that than live without her.

"New wounded," a corpsman called.

Jenny walked out of the dispensary just in time to see a direct hit on CCS number three's surgery. A large cloud of black and red smoke climbed into the air, hung there for a moment, then spewed pieces of people and things in a wide circle. Stunned and unmoving, Jenny recognized two bodies falling through the smoke into the mud below.

Rebecca Willis ran past her. "Kincade, stay here. Phillips and Peters, come with me."

She watched as the three women ran toward the human debris.

"I can't stop the bleeding, Lieutenant." A corpsman's voice brought Jenny back to triage at number fourteen.

Later that night she learned that a surgeon, his patient, and two nurses had been killed when the shell struck CCS number three.

"The loss of life would have been much greater if they hadn't been closed for three hours," Rebecca said.

140

The thought of what might have been sent chills through Jenny's body.

CHAPTER 24

There was no progress in the landing site over the next two weeks. The Germans kept their vantage point in the Alban hills, able to see the entire beachhead, effectively slowing the allied advance to a dead stop. The casualty toll was more than anyone had expected. There was no letup in the supply of newly wounded men.

At night Jenny would lie on her cot, her body too tired to move, her mind too keyed up to sleep. She had learned to ignore the shelling, but she could never let go of the fear it engendered in her.

There's no safe place on Anzio beach, Jenny thought. The front lines don't draw so much fire. If we have to dig in any deeper we'll turn into moles. What good is it anyway? They can't put the hospital far enough underground to protect it. No wonder the men have nicknamed it "hell's little acre." Every wounded soldier brought in here for treatment has an excellent chance of being wounded while they're receiving treatment.

"I'm beginning to think we'll spend the rest of the war stuck on this beach," Rebecca Willis grumbled. Jenny watched her as she wiped at her face with a small tan towel. Mud and several beetles had become part of the cold cream Rebecca had spread over her face. "Damn these bugs. I wish they'd stay out of things."

Jenny laughed.

"What's so funny?"

"It just seems strange to be more concerned about the bugs than you are about the artillery," Jenny replied.

"I haven't found an artillery shell in my cold cream lately," Rebecca said. "I can't say the same for the beetles."

"They're probably wondering what people are doing living in five-foot holes. They're probably just as put out as we are."

"I'm not impressed, Jenny. I'd gladly give them back their homes. I'm tired of living in mud."

"I know what you mean. I dropped a thermometer this morning and it disappeared before I could grab it. I never did find it."

Shells burst overhead and several explosives could be heard in the direction of the convoy.

"I've forgotten what it's like to be in a place that's actually quiet at night. Listen to that racket," Rebecca fumed. "If it's not the planes, the guns or the bombs, it's the Lorries running up and down the beach all night like the night creatures from a horror movie, prowling from sundown to sun up."

"I used to think I'd get so tired I'd eventually have to fall asleep," Jenny said. "I forgot about staying asleep." She brushed her hand through her hair, knocking clouds of fine dust from it. "Between the mud and the dust I feel like I should be condemned as a health hazard. Maybe I should have listened to my father. He told me women didn't belong in combat."

"Haven't you heard?" Rebecca said, mocking. "We're not in combat. We don't carry guns, and we don't go in until the beach has been secured. So . . . we're non-combatants."

"You went in with the first assault wave in North Africa," Jenny pointed out. "Besides, first wave, or tenth wave, we've been under fire since we landed here."

"Tell it to the American people," Rebecca said. "We British have been living in a war zone since nineteen thirty-nine. The American male likes to think of his women as safe and protected." She shrugged. "Beats me what they think you nurses are doing out here. We see more of the horror of combat in one day than most G.I.'s or Tommies see in a month."

"You'll get no argument from me. But I doubt that you'll ever convince the American people. They have no category for women living and working under combat conditions. They'd rather keep their fantasies about nurses in starched white dresses, walking peacefully onto a secure beachhead, with the front lines at least seven miles away."

"Humph," Rebecca said. "I've been in three landings and I haven't seen a secure beach yet."

A shell exploded overhead, and for a minute the ground shook with the concussion.

"Is anybody home?" a woman's voice called. Jenny turned to see Phyllis Dodd, one of the senior nurses, side-stepping down the wooden stairs.

"What are you doing out at night?" Rebecca asked. "You trying to get yourself killed?"

"I need a cot for the night," Phyllis Dodd said. "The walls of our tent caved in. The men can't rebuild until morning. Susan and Deborah are staying in Rachel's tent. Her mates are working night shift."

"Help yourself." Rebecca pointed toward the empty cot. "The walls probably won't fall in on you, but I can't speak for the beetles."

"Listen, I'm so tired nothing could keep me awake," Phyllis Dodd said as she stretched out on the cot.

Rebecca pulled the rough military blanket over her shoulders and looked at Jenny. "You'd better get some sleep too — while it's quiet."

"Some quiet." Jenny snuggled into the blanket. It smelled of rain and mildew and scratched against her skin.

The harsh realities of Anzio faded as she turned her thoughts to Maggie. Maggie, spotlessly clean in fresh khakis and butter-soft flight jacket, holding her close, smelling of soap and morning rain. She took a deep breath and remembered the softness of Maggie's mouth.

145

She prayed silently. Dear God, don't let anything happen to us before I tell her how much I love her and want to share her life. Please, God, don't let us suffer that.

CHAPTER 25

Jenny held her helmet on with one hand as she ran from her tent to the receiving station. Stretchers were lined up four and five deep forming a human wall around the dispensary. Night shift nurses were making their way through the triage area. She ducked into headquarter's tent where the Chief Matron had already begun the shift transfer.

"As you can see by our stretcher cases, the Germans hit our boys hard last night. Intelligence says it's the beginning of a new German offensive."

The Matron's face grew even more serious. "We lost a hospital ship last night."

The tent became perfectly quiet. Jenny could feel the tension stretch across the room.

The Chief Matron continued, "Two German planes bombed the Leinster and the Saint David. The Leinster was not badly hit. It made it to port with its casualties." She cleared her throat. "The Saint David was not so lucky. It received a direct hit and had only six minutes to disembark the wounded before it sank. The Sisters were still on board when her bow began to rise steeply and she slid down stern first."

A wave of sorrow, anger and fear splashed around the tent. "I'm told it was the Captain who ordered the boats to wait for the Sisters. Most of them jumped into the sea and were picked up by the Leinster and the Saint Andrew. The Captain, the RAMC Commanding Officer, the Chief Matron, and three Sisters went down with the ship."

The group sat in total silence. A family tragedy had been announced, its cost and meaning undeniable. Tears filled the Chief Matron's eyes.

Rebecca Willis leaned toward Jenny. She whispered, "Her sister was Chief Matron on the Saint David."

"Keep them in your prayers tonight," the Chief Matron said. Again, her voice hardened with efficiency. "The assignments for today: Willis, Gold and Kincade, relieve night shift in triage. Don't wait for the end of the meeting. You can go now."

Jenny, flanked by three stretcher teams and two corpsmen, stepped quickly between the rows of wounded. She knelt in the mud and examined the first patient.

"Am I going to lose my leg?" the young soldier asked. He clutched Jenny's hand, his fingers pressing into her flesh. His eyes were glossy, a response to the morphine injection the corpsman had given him. "I'd rather die than lose my leg."

Jenny brushed his hair back from his face. "We'll do everything we can," she said. "Let me take a look." Bending over the bloody leg, she cut the pants leg away. Jenny's hand stopped in mid-motion as the rancid smell of rotting flesh rose to meet her. "Gas gangrene. He's next." She tied a priority tag around the ankle on the uninjured leg.

"No!" the soldier shouted. "Don't take my leg. Don't take my leg."

There was no time for comfort. Lives depended on speed and judgment. She moved from one wounded man to the next. The acrid odor of blood and burned flesh penetrated her nostrils and mouth. The sickening odor of necrotic tissue mixed with the blood and burns threatened to turn Jenny's stomach. She swallowed hard, fighting the urge to vomit, refusing to give it her attention or time.

Three hours later the triage area was clear. The wounded had been dispatched for treatment and Jenny, too tired to move, sat on a partially sunken cinder block. She watched the activity in front of the post-operative tent where Rebecca was directing a stretcher team inside.

Suddenly, she was aware of the sound of a plane's engine. It stood out against the relative calm and drew Jenny's gaze upward. Fear shot through her. It was a German plane, and it was starting to descend for a run at the Casualty Clearing Station. She looked again at the post-operative tent. Two

149

stretchers had been laid on cinder blocks by the entrance. She looked back at the plane. Its wings tilted left, then right, as the pilot drew his course for the beach. My God, Jenny thought, terrified. The bastard is going to strafe the post-op tent. He'll kill those patients.

She ran toward the two stretchers, her legs heavy as her feet disappeared in the mud and splashed it against her woolen military slacks. She heard the sound of the plane's cannons and glanced over her shoulder as she ran. Fiery tracers had left the plane's guns and were moving toward the beach. They looked like long ribbons of fire as they sliced into the mud.

Her lungs were burning as she pushed herself to run faster. Her heart thudded in her ears.

The sounds of the plane were louder now. She saw Rebecca Willis come to the entrance of the post-op tent and stand motionless.

"No!" Jenny screamed. "Rebecca, get back."

Red streamers were falling around her. Mud splashed into the air and fell back with a plopping sound.

She and the tracers were several feet from the tent. She watched in horror as bloody holes appeared at every point where the tracers disappeared into Rebecca's body. Rebecca crumpled and collapsed into the mud like a rag doll.

Jenny threw herself at one of the stretchers, knocking the wounded and unconscious man onto the ground and into the tent. The air was filled with the sounds of shells entering the mud around her.

She turned and reached for the second wounded man. It was too late. Long lines of fire were moving directly at her. There was nowhere to run. Something jagged and hot tore at her flesh. I'm hit, she thought. I wonder if I'll die.

Pain became her only reality. She was vaguely aware that the plane had banked into a turn and was coming around for a second pass. She was on her knees now, the mud was soft, cold, and red. I'm bleeding. I have to get the soldier before I pass out.

She crawled toward the second wounded man and with one enormous effort pulled the stretcher to the ground. His body fell sideways and rolled toward the tent.

The plane's engines were louder now. Tracers filled the air — long strings of flames falling to earth like rain. Something sharp and hot hit her in the face. Pain shot through her head.

Oh God, she thought. Let Maggie know the truth.

She caught herself on both hands as her body fell forward into the mud.

"Maggie," she whispered. "Maggie."

Pain possessed her completely and pulled her into unconsciousness.

CHAPTER 26

"Hi," Maggie said as Christine opened the door to her flat. "You sounded very serious on the phone. What's up?"

Christine, her face a mixture of sadness and concern, sat on the sofa next to Maggie.

Maggie took the initiative. "If you're worried that I'm still mad at you for not telling me about Jenny's company being shipped out, forget it. Besides, I should have my clearance for Anzio in another week. I can work things out with Jenny in person."

Christine cleared her throat. "Maggie, David called me this morning. He wanted to have lunch. I met him at a pub."

Maggie fumed anger at the mention of David's name. "It's your business, Chris, but I don't understand how you can be friends with a blackmailer. After what he did to Jenny and me, how can you trust him?"

"I don't trust him," Christine said. "He said he had something important to tell me. I went to lunch out of curiosity."

"Unless it directly affects Jenny, I don't care what it is." Maggie could feel the heat in her face and the blood in her temples.

"I think you'd better hear this. It's about Jenny."

Maggie's heartbeat increased. "What about Jenny? Is she all right?" She was afraid of Christine's response.

"Jenny's been seriously wounded. She's in the hospital at Blasingstoke."

Christine's words hit Maggie like a hammer. She felt the room spin, and for a second she couldn't catch her breath.

"What happened? Will she be all right? I need to go see her," Maggie stammered. Thoughts and feelings collided inside her and made it difficult to think clearly.

Christine put her hand on Maggie's shoulder. "For a while the doctors thought they'd have to amputate her right leg." Christine paused. "They managed to save it, but she'll walk with a limp from now on."

Suddenly Maggie remembered the specialty at Blasingstoke. "There has to be something else or she

153

wouldn't be at Blasingstoke. What is it?" She dreaded Christine's answer.

"Shrapnel tore her face up badly. According to David she'll need twenty or thirty surgeries to restore it. They can't start reconstruction until she's in better condition to withstand the procedures."

Maggie felt as if a giant hand had turned her world upside down. The thought of Jenny's pain was almost too much to bear. She wanted to run to her, to comfort her, to take her pain away. "I have to see her. I'll go to Blasingstoke today." She started to get up. Christine pulled her back.

"Wait a minute, Maggie." Christine kept her hand on Maggie's arm. "David is on emergency leave. He's staying near the hospital. There's no way he'll allow you to see Jenny."

"Then why did he tell you?" Maggie was furious at David. "He had to know you'd tell me."

"I'm not sure it crossed his mind. He said he couldn't stand another day of being cooped up in a hospital room. David never has been one to feel much compassion for the sick or wounded. I was surprised to learn he'd been at the hospital for ten days. It's my guess he doesn't want to look bad to his commanding officer."

Maggie exploded. "I don't give a damn what he wants. I'm going to see Jenny. I'll be on my way as soon as I can get a car."

Christine got up and walked to the door with Maggie. "There's nothing I can say that will stop you?"

"No."

Christine took her uniform jacket from the hall closet. "I suspected as much. I'm going with you. If I can't stop you, maybe I can keep you out of trouble." She opened the door. "I have a car parked about a block from here."

Maggie felt the warm friendship in Christine's words. "Thanks, Chris. I really appreciate it."

CHAPTER 27

Maggie paced the waiting area while a Sister went to inform David that his wife had visitors. Five minutes later David appeared in the doorway. His eyes focused on Maggie and his face turned scarlet.

"Why did you bring her here, Christine?" David demanded. "Get her out of here before I kill her."

Maggie was determined. "I'm not leaving until I see Jenny." She glared at David.

"You're not going to see Jenny. Not now, not ever." David's eyes narrowed to tiny slits. His cadence had the rhythm of a machine gun. "If you know

what's good for you, you'll leave while you still can."
He raised a fist at her. "I'd like nothing better than
to beat the hell out of you. If you don't leave, I may
do exactly that."

Maggie knew only one thing: she would see Jenny
whether he liked it or not. She started to walk
around him toward Jenny's room. David grabbed her
arm and spun her around. His fist was drawn back,
ready to strike.

"David." Christine's voice was sharp, cold and
controlling.

He dropped his arm. "I won't hit the bitch, but
get her out of my sight. It makes me sick to look at
her."

Christine stepped between them. "If you both
continue like this, we'll all be asked to leave. Is that
what you want for Jenny? To embarrass her with the
nurses and hospital staff?"

Christine was right. Maggie pulled her arm away
from David. "Let me see her for five minutes and I'll
leave."

"Not for five seconds," David hissed through
clenched teeth.

"I won't leave until she knows I'm here."

"David, please let her see Jenny so we can go
back to London," Christine said.

"No." His word was like a slap. But after a stern
look from Christine he relented. "I'll ask Jenny if she
wants to see you. If she says yes, you can go in."

He disappeared down the hall. In five minutes he
returned.

Maggie took several steps toward David as he
reached the doorway of the waiting area. She glared
at him. She hated the self-satisfied look on his face.

"Now will you go? Or do I have to call the M.P.s to throw you off the base?" David taunted.

"You bastard," Maggie said. She watched as the corners of David's mouth twisted into a sneer. Her hands were shaking and she fought the desire to hit David.

He turned toward Christine. "If this . . . *thing* means anything to you, you'd better get her out of here now."

Christine put her hand on Maggie's arm. "We're finished here, Maggie. Let's go home."

CHAPTER 28

There had never been a doubt in Jenny's mind that she wanted to recover from her wounds. She had fought for life with the fervor of a soldier on the battlefield. For the first several weeks after her injuries, she had remained in the soft haze of painkillers and sedatives. With time, the injections came less frequently and she grew increasingly aware of the nature of her wounds.

The crisis about her leg had come and gone without her knowledge. The doctor seemed overjoyed when he informed her that she would walk with a pronounced limp but would not have to lose her leg. She accepted the news resolutely. I suppose I can live with that, she thought. It was the bandages on her face that concerned her now.

She had looked about the room for a mirror, and, finding none, had examined the bandage with her hand. The entire right side of her face was encased in padded gauze. She could feel the pressure of her fingers as she cautiously explored the bandage. This isn't good, she thought. There must be a lot of damage.

Her doctor wouldn't say much at first. He continued a litany delivered one message at a time. None of them made Jenny feel better about her wounds. He was careful, however, to remind her that it would require many operations before her face could be repaired. "You shouldn't expect too much at first," he told her. "Your face has suffered a serious insult."

Jenny thought about those words each night while she lay awake in her darkened room. Why not just say, you'll be disfigured for life?

She thought of Maggie, too. How she could no longer plan a life with her. She loved her too much to saddle her with a monstrous cripple. If it were just her leg, she could risk it. A lot of people would limp when this war was over. But she couldn't stand it if Maggie saw her face and turned away in disgust. That pain would be worse than any wound the Germans could inflict. And if she didn't turn away, how could Jenny know it wasn't pity that kept Maggie with her? She couldn't do that to them. It would destroy even their memories. Somehow, she would have to live without Maggie. Somehow, she must never let Maggie know the extent of her love.

The test of her resolve had come faster than she had expected. She had not thought Maggie would find her so quickly. She had not considered that David might ask if she wanted to see Maggie. She was surprised by his question, but her decision not to see Maggie had been made long before today.

She had listened to David's footsteps walk away from her. She could imagine Maggie's pain when he told her. Better that kind of pain than pity, she thought. In time, she'd find someone else. Someone whole. Someone she wouldn't have to pity.

* * * * *

She heard the door open and David's footsteps come toward her bed.

"They're gone." He looked down at her. "Are you crying?"

She felt his hand brush the tears from her cheek.

"Are you worried about tomorrow? I can arrange to be here if you insist. There's still time to rearrange my appointments." His voice sounded as insincere as his words.

Jenny looked at him. His face was no longer handsome to her. "That's not necessary. I'll have Doctor Samuels and Sister Greenfield. I won't need you."

"If you're sure you'll be all right . . ."

Jenny was tired of David's pretense. Her anger flared as she again watched the coldness in his eyes. "Why don't you stop this act? It's not necessary for

161

you to be here at all. Do us both a favor. Go back to your ship."

David reddened. "You act as if I don't care at all. That's not true. I don't like seeing you like this. It's demeaning to both of us."

She felt a quick stab of pain at the message behind his words. She wanted him out. Out of her room and out of her life. "Don't say another word. Just get the hell out of here. If you won't go back to your ship, at least leave for tonight. I'm sick of listening to you."

His words were a hiss between clenched teeth. "Do you think I like sitting here all day looking at those bandages? You know I don't like being around sick people. Even the smell of this place makes me sick." His voice softened. "I'm trying, Jenny. I really am. I'm sorry I'm not the strong, heroic type you thought you were marrying. I wish I could change, but I can't. I do the best I can. I love you."

Jenny's face had begun to throb with the rush of her anger. She touched her bandage lightly as pain shot through the right side of her face. He's not worth this, she thought. Why argue with him? She took a deep breath. "Let's not fight anymore. I'm tired of battles."

David leaned toward her. "I don't want to fight either. I care about you, Jenny. If I seem distracted, it's because I'm trying to rethink our future. You aren't going to be able to work. You won't even be able to be the kind of hostess I'll need when this war is over." He took a deep breath. "But I'm willing to overlook all that. Somehow we'll manage. But you'll have to be patient with me. This isn't what I planned

162

for my life. I don't like the idea that people will always see us as different."

"It's too late for us, David." Jenny was contemptuous of David's feeble attempt at reconciliation. "I no longer care what other people think. Anzio changed my mind about a lot of things. I don't think you and I will be together too much longer." The little pity she had once felt for him had all but disappeared. "You really don't have to be here. I don't expect you to be."

David fidgeted in his chair. "My friends and commanding officer expect it. Besides, you're going to need some help. I'm willing to try to help you through this. Why don't you give me some credit?"

Jenny was exhausted. "David, right now I'm too tired to give anybody anything. Please leave so I can sleep."

CHAPTER 29

The surgeon was delayed by an emergency and didn't reach Jenny's room until twelve-thirty in the afternoon. He unwrapped the bandages from her face as carefully as if she was a delicate piece of crystal.

"It's doing very nicely," Doctor Samuels said. He ran his fingertips gently over the wounds. "We should be able to start your surgeries in a month or so."

"That's good," Jenny said. She looked directly at him. "I'd like to see what I look like. Could I have a mirror, please?"

She watched as Sister Greenfield exchanged glances with the surgeon. He nodded.

"I'll get you a mirror," Sister Greenfield said, walking quickly from the room.

"I want you to remember that we can reconstruct your face. It will take time and it won't be perfect, but it can be done," Doctor Samuels said. His expression was kind and concerned.

Jenny felt a surge of fear. "It must really look bad."

"I've seen and rebuilt a lot worse."

There was a knock on the door, and it opened immediately. Doctor Samuels and Jenny turned toward the sound expecting to see Sister Greenfield with a mirror in her hand. Instead they saw David.

He looked toward Jenny and stopped mid-stride. His eyes grew large, his smile disappeared, and a look of disgust crossed his ashen face. "My God," he said, obviously horror-stricken. "I had no idea . . ."

Sister Greenfield spoke from behind him. "If you'll wait outside, Lieutenant, I'll call you when the doctor is finished."

David turned and left in stunned silence. Sister Greenfield walked to the bed and handed the mirror to Jenny. Jenny held it with the mirror side down. "I'm not so sure now that I want to look." Her heart was pounding and her mouth was dry with anxiety.

"You might as well," Sister Greenfield said. "Don't let your husband's reaction decide for you."

Jenny inhaled deeply, turned the mirror toward herself, and looked at her reflection. She drew in her breath sharply and closed her eyes. "No wonder David acted like that," she said. "I don't look human." She forced herself to look again. This

165

couldn't be real. Nothing could repair this. A jagged red line ran from the corner of her mouth and stopped just under her eye. Another line, more jagged and red than the other, started on the side of her nose, curled around the corner of her eye, and extended almost to her hairline. Two equally deep and jagged horizontal wounds crossed under her eye and extended to the top of her ear. A large depression was visible in her cheek just below the junction of the three intersecting wounds. A large flap of skin had been lifted from her face by the shrapnel and had been sewn back by medics.

Jenny dropped the mirror on the bed and wiped at her tears.

"We can reconstruct it, Jenny," Doctor Samuels said. He laid his hand on Jenny's shoulder, replaced the dressing, patted Jenny on the head, and left to continue his rounds.

"Should I tell your husband to come in?" Sister Greenfield asked. She was a large woman, tall, with orange red hair that stuck from beneath her cap like frayed wires. She was heavy, soft and rounded like a balloon with a slow leak. "Maybe you should wait until tomorrow to talk with him. I don't think you need his childish dramatics. If it's all right with you, I'll tell him we gave you a sedative and he could come back tomorrow."

"I'd appreciate that," Jenny said. "I'm really not in the mood to see him right now."

CHAPTER 30

David carried Jenny's suitcase to the car. It was her first furlough from the hospital. She would have two weeks to relax before the next surgery on her face. No one but a plastic surgeon would be able to see any difference in Jenny's appearance following this three-hour operation, the first of many. The bandages were not as thick as before, but they still covered a large portion of her face. Doctor Samuels had told Jenny that the bandage was no longer necessary, but she had chosen to keep it in order to hide her scars.

David's visits had grown short and infrequent over the past six weeks. When he was at the hospital, he was sullen and withdrawn. Jenny had not pushed him for an explanation or asked him the reason for his reticence. She knew only too well that the change in him was linked directly to his accidental look at her scars. It hadn't mattered enough to her to coax him into conversation. In truth, she was more comfortable with his silence than his constant sarcasm.

They had driven thirty miles toward London in virtual silence. David appeared more withdrawn than usual. Jenny was tired of the tension, tired of the sham David had forced on her.

"I'm worried about you, David," Jenny said. "You're not as cutting and sarcastic as you used to be. What's on your mind?"

"We'd better not get into it," he baited. "It would only upset you."

Frustrated by David's refusal to communicate, she said, "Whatever it is, I'd feel better if you just got it out."

He sighed. "I guess you're right. The truth can't do any more damage than already's been done."

She felt her muscles tense, and watched David closely.

"The truth is," he began, "I'm absolutely devastated."

She was shocked. Of all the things he might have said, she hadn't expected this.

David's fingers were drumming against the steering wheel. "I know how bad this is going to sound," he continued, "but I can't help it."

"Go on."

"I don't know if I can deal with your wounds. I hate what they've done to you. Every time I see you limp across a room, I want to scream. Every time I hear the tapping sound of your cane, I want to scream at the injustice of it." His voice quivered slightly. "It's not fair. Why should this happen to me? It's as if God wants to punish you, and because I'm with you, I get punished too. All my life I've had an image of the girl who would be my wife. You used to be that girl." He took another deep breath. "It nevaer occurred to me that your face might be destroyed."

Jenny stumbled under the blow and fought to regain her emotional balance. She was furious with herself and angry with David. She strained to control her voice. "I should have left you months ago. I should never have gone back with you after Christmas. All I could think about were your threats. They seem awfully unimportant right now. In fact, I don't give a damn what you do. Go to my C.O. if you like. A dishonorable discharge would be better than putting up with you."

"You're forgetting your girlfriend."

"I haven't forgotten anything. Maggie Conover no longer concerns me. She didn't even put up a fight for us. As far as I'm concerned, she's as bad as you are. I'm sick of both of you. I don't give a damn what you do to her or her career." She hoped David would believe her.

"Wait a minute. You don't run this marriage, I do. I want a divorce as much as you do, but not until the war is over and my career is established. We can live apart, have our own lives, and wait until the time is right. I can tell everyone you're in the States for surgery. That way neither one of us is embarrassed."

"You bastard. The hell with your career." She couldn't believe David's insensitivity. The right side of her face was throbbing wildly. "You can drop me off at the hotel. After that I never want to see you again. I'll file for divorce on Monday. If you object, I'll tell the court what you're like in bed. Wait until you see what that can do to your precious career."

"You wouldn't do that."

"Don't kid yourself, David." Jenny's voice was filled with contempt. "I no longer care what happens to me. If you have any sense at all, you'll drop me at the hotel and say good-bye."

CHAPTER 31

The hotel lobby was crowded with military personnel checking in and out. It was the usual weekend crowd, intent on a good time.

Overly self-conscious as she walked from the main entrance to the registration desk, Jenny leaned heavily on her cane, its usual tapping sound muffled by the deep wine carpet. She avoided eye contact and kept her focus on the large grandfather clock to the right of the desk. The Westminster chimes struck noon.

She registered for the room David had reserved. "Could you have someone take my suitcase up? It's the brown leather bag just inside the front door."

The clerk glanced down at her cane. "I can carry it up for you. Just give me a minute."

"Thank you. I'm going to stop in the bar."

Jenny was still reeling with the sting of David's remarks. Maybe a drink will help my nerves, she thought.

The bar was crowded, but she found a table in a dimly lit corner. She ordered a brandy and settled back in her chair. She was unaccustomed to alcohol, and the drink relaxed her immediately. She was too exhausted to think.

"Jenny."

The sound of her name startled her. She turned her head and saw Maggie standing beside the table.

"Maggie." She was completely taken by surprise. "What are you doing here?"

"Looking for you," Maggie said. "I need to talk with you." She pulled out a chair without waiting for an invitation.

"How did you know I was here? We're blocks from the Savoy." She felt awkward in front of Maggie and moved her cane out of sight. "You couldn't have known."

"I've known for two weeks that you'd be checking into the hotel today. I've been keeping up with you since the day David sent me away from Blasingstoke." She leaned forward. "Did you really expect me to just forget about you?" Her voice was like velvet. "I can't do that, Jenny. I love you too much."

Jenny tried to ignore her desire for Maggie's arms around her. "You wasted your time," she said. "I have nothing to offer."

"I haven't asked for anything except your time. I have to know why you won't leave David. Why I — why *we* — don't mean enough to you to take that chance."

Two sailors brushed by their table.

"This isn't the place to talk," Jenny said. Her eyes are bluer than I remembered, she thought.

"All right," Maggie said. "You name the place. But when you do, know that if you don't meet me, I'll show up again at Blasingstoke. And I won't leave until you do talk to me." Maggie kept her eyes on Jenny's face.

She recognized the determination in Maggie's eyes. "I believe you would." She picked up her cane and stood up. "We might as well get it over with. We can talk in my room."

Maggie looked down at her watch. "David's been gone forty minutes. Will he be back soon?"

"He won't be back at all. I'm filing for a divorce on Monday."

CHAPTER 32

There was a small conversation area in front of the bed. Maggie seated herself in the over-stuffed chair and watched Jenny make her way to the sofa opposite her. Her limp was more pronounced without the background of the hotel crowd. Maggie's thoughts traveled back to Jenny walking on the beach at Brighton — healthy, graceful and confident.

Jenny's eyes looked everywhere except at Maggie. She rested her cane against the side of the sofa and was still, as if gathering strength.

She waited patiently for Jenny to focus on her. When she did, Maggie smiled. "It's good to see you," Maggie said. "I was afraid you'd return to the States without letting me know." She paused, watching Jenny's eyes. "I would have followed you, of course."

"What good would that have done? I've told you that we have no future together. Why must you persist?"

"I have to, Jenny. I'm still in love with you."

Jenny looked at her. "I've changed, Maggie. I'm not as naive as I used to be. I no longer believe that every story has a happy ending, or that justice always wins out. I know better now. I don't have as much control over my life as I once did. I can make decisions all right, but my decisions don't always lead where I thought they would." She paused. "I guess that could pass for a degree of wisdom in some circles."

"And the bitterness?" Maggie asked.

Jenny's eyes darkened. "I don't like the changes my injuries have brought into my life, the changes they continue to bring. It's selfish, but at times I wish I could change places with someone who made it through Anzio unscathed."

"I'd feel the same way. Most people would." Maggie wanted to hold Jenny, to feel her close, to comfort her. "I don't think I'd believe anyone who said they were glad it was them instead of the soldier or nurse standing next to them. Anzio must have been hell."

Jenny felt the love in Maggie's voice. It was the most comforting thing she had experienced in months. "It was a nightmare. You can't imagine. No one could unless they were there. I don't think I've ever seen doctors and nurses as exhausted as we were. We pushed ourselves through what we had to do. Sheer willpower. But even that gave out eventually. People just collapsed where they stood."

She touched the edge of her bandage. "When the plane came in to strafe and bomb the station, I couldn't believe my eyes. There was no place to hide."

"Like you're hiding now?" Maggie asked. "Am I the reason you and David are getting a divorce?"

"No. You have nothing to do with it." Jenny was emphatic. "Our marriage was a mistake from the first day. It died of its own weight."

"And what about us, Jenny? Are we dead, too?"

"Whatever we had is gone. It was exciting while it lasted, but nothing lasts forever. It's time we both got on with our lives."

"I love you and I want you back," Maggie insisted. "I'm miserable without you." She leaned toward Jenny and fought her desire to take her in her arms.

"It wouldn't work, Maggie. I'm too damaged. I'll be a cripple the rest of my life. I'm still facing years of surgery. The doctors hope they can rebuild my face, but who knows? Life doesn't give guarantees."

"I'm not asking for guarantees," Maggie said. "I just want to be with you." Maggie felt her heart would break. "Nothing changes my feelings for you. I'm in love with you, Jenny. I want you to share my life. I want you to plan a future with me. I want to fall asleep with my arms around you each night, and wake up with you every morning."

"You're not thinking this through, Maggie. You could be saddled with a disfigured cripple for life.

176

Eventually you'd start to hate me. Or even worse, you'd stay with me out of pity. I couldn't live with either." Jenny's voice cracked.

"I don't pity you. I love you. You got a rotten break. It happens in wars." Her eyes and voice softened. "I want you because I'm in love with you. Gladly and hopelessly in love with you. I need you, Jenny. Nothing tastes good without you. Please give us another chance."

"Maggie, you haven't seen my face. I don't look human anymore. I'm a monstrosity. Even if it can be repaired in time, it will never be right. And even that will take years. Years, Maggie. Years you'd be living with someone who has half a face." She searched Maggie's eyes. "You don't know how bad it is."

"Then show me," Maggie said. "Take the bandage off so I can see for myself. If I have to lose you, I want to know why."

"I want you to remember my face the way it was before Anzio." There was growing panic in Jenny's voice.

"That's not good enough," Maggie said. "You owe me the right to make my own decisions. I want to see your face, Jenny."

"It will only make things worse," she pleaded.

"Show me, Jenny. Show me what you're afraid for me to see."

Tears formed in Jenny's eyes. Her hands reached to the bandage and worked the corners free. She pulled it slowly away from her skin, holding it in place like a shield. Then, with a deep breath and a quick move of her hands, she lowered the bandage to her lap. Her eyes were frightened and resigned. She waited in silence as if bracing herself for the verbal blow she feared would come.

Maggie looked slowly along Jenny's face, pausing for a moment on the jagged edges of the deep red scars before returning again to Jenny's eyes.

She slid from her chair, knelt at Jenny's feet, and took Jenny's hands into her own. Without a word she raised the slender hands to her lips and kissed each palm. She was filled with tenderness.

"I'm looking at you, Jenny . . . and all I see is the woman I love, the woman I want to share my life with. All I see is you." She kissed Jenny's eyes lightly, brushed her lips along the scars. She kissed Jenny's lips, tasting the salt of tears. Her hand moved to Jenny's face, gentle fingers tracing the path that the shrapnel had taken.

She was overcome with love for Jenny, completely enveloped, totally absorbed in feelings. Her heart raced as her love rose like a flame, moving upward, enfolding her in its heart.

Jenny's lips were warm and soft. They opened willingly to accept her inside. Her tongue moved slowly against the sweetness of Jenny's mouth. Her arms encircled Jenny and pulled her close. She could feel Jenny's breasts firm against her own.

"I love you, Jenny," Maggie whispered through a kiss.

She felt the heat of Jenny's mouth pulling her forward, drawing her inside. She was filled with love and passion long denied — a longing for Jenny that would not die.

* * * * *

178

Jenny's desire ignited from within as Maggie kissed and caressed her into nakedness. Waves of excitement washed over her as the warmth of Maggie's fingers slipped beneath her bra and traced the heated passion in her nipples. She inhaled sharply as Maggie feathered kisses along the curve of her hip and down her thighs. Tenderness merged with passion as the tip of Maggie's tongue grazed the satin pearl.

"I want you so much, Jenny." Maggie's breath was warm against the red crisscross of scars left by shrapnel in the pale skin of her leg.

She bent down to meet Maggie's hot kisses as they rose upward, leaving bright fires burning in their wake. She took possession of Maggie's mouth, covering Maggie's lips with her kiss, matching the strokes of Maggie's tongue, plunging herself deep inside Maggie's mouth.

"I love you, Maggie." Her tongue brushed Maggie's lips. "Make love to me."

Maggie's arms felt strong as they lifted her. She felt Maggie's heart beat against the softness of her own breast as she was carried to bed.

Jenny sighed deeply as Maggie's body covered her . . . skin against skin . . . silk upon silk . . . making contact at every possible point.

Maggie's kisses felt hotter now. They spoke love and tenderness, passion and desire. Maggie's lips grazed her hair, her eyes, her cheek. They lingered on the jagged scars of her face, embracing and accepting them.

Maggie's lips were an imperceptible weight — a warm soft presence — speaking love with her touch, desire with her tongue. She entered Jenny's mouth with the subtlety of time, exchanging absence for presence.

She shivered as the warmth of Maggie's mouth moved along the curve of her neck, across her shoulder, and engulfed her breast. Nipples firm with excitement grew more rigid with increasing passion. She pushed her fingers into the soft curls of Maggie's hair and guided Maggie's head gently upward. There was no resistance as she sucked Maggie's tongue deep inside herself.

"I love you," she moaned into Maggie's mouth, following with the heat of her tongue. "I've wanted you so."

She gasped as Maggie trailed kisses down her body, stopping only to caress her breasts, to take her nipples between her teeth, to embrace them in the warm wetness of her mouth. She wanted Maggie more than she had ever wanted anyone. Her body ached with longing. She opened her legs and guided Maggie's head gently downward. Kisses flowed like liquid fire against her skin, searing her body to its core, igniting her heart and soul.

"Oh . . ." A long deep sigh escaped Jenny's lips as Maggie's tongue moved between her thighs. She felt its softness gliding and caressing. Excitement raced through her body as Maggie sucked her gently into her mouth. Pleasure intensified. It moved like a gathering storm, collecting strength as it grew, sweeping her into its heart.

Jenny let go, moaning to the rhythm of Maggie's tongue. A scream filled the room. It lifted her and exploded, spiralling her into ecstasy. All boundaries disappeared. Time fell away.

* * * * *

They lay in each other's arms, comfortable in each other's keeping.

"Where are you?" Jenny asked. "You look a thousand miles away." She ran her fingertips across Maggie's lips.

Maggie kissed Jenny's fingers and wrapped them inside her hand. "I was thinking of a line from Gibran's *Prophet*." She looked deeply into Jenny's eyes. " 'And think not you can direct the course of love, for love, if it finds you worthy, directs your course.' " She kissed Jenny.

"I don't know what David will do, Maggie. He could still destroy us."

"I'll take my chances," Maggie replied. "I can face anything as long as you're with me."

"I love you," Jenny said. "I'll be with you as long as you want me."

"Always." They kissed again and each surrendered to love's direction.

In reclaiming women's history, their contribution during World War II is frequently overlooked. Here are the statistics in this area:

More than one hundred military nurses were captured when Batan and Corregidor fell to the Japanese. Sixty-six Army Nurses and eleven Navy Nurses remained in a Japanese concentration camp for thirty-seven months.

Sixteen hundred Army Nurses and five hundred and sixty-five WACs received combat decorations, including Distinguished Service Medals, Silver Stars, Bronze Stars, Air Medals, Legions of Merit, Commendation Medals, and Purple Hearts.

During the battle of Anzio, six Army Nurses were killed by German bombing, strafing and shelling of the tented hospital area. Four Army Nurses among the survivors were awarded Silver Stars for extraordinary courage under fire.

In all, more than two hundred Army Nurses lost their lives during World War II. Seventeen of those valiant women are buried in American cemeteries in foreign lands.

A few of the publications of
THE NAIAD PRESS, INC.
P.O. Box 10543 • Tallahassee, Florida 32302
Phone (904) 539-5965
Toll-Free Order Number: 1-800-533-1973
Mail orders welcome. Please include 15% postage.

PAXTON COURT by Diane Salvatore. 256 pp. Erotic and wickedly funny contemporary tale about the business of learning to live together. ISBN 1-56280-109-0 $21.95

PAYBACK by Celia Cohen. 176 pp. A gripping thriller of romance, revenge and betrayal. ISBN 1-56280-084-1 10.95

THE BEACH AFFAIR by Barbara Johnson. 224 pp. Sizzling summer romance/mystery/intrigue. ISBN 1-56280-090-6 10.95

GETTING THERE by Robbi Sommers. 192 pp. Nobody does it like Robbi! ISBN 1-56280-099-X 10.95

FINAL CUT by Lisa Haddock. 208 pp. 2nd Carmen Ramirez mystery. ISBN 1-56280-088-4 10.95

FLASHPOINT by Katherine V. Forrest. 256 pp. A Lesbian blockbuster! ISBN 1-56280-079-5 10.95

DAUGHTERS OF A CORAL DAWN by Katherine V. Forrest. Audio Book — read by Jane Merrow. ISBN 1-56280-110-4 16.95

CLAIRE OF THE MOON by Nicole Conn. Audio Book —Read by Marianne Hyatt. ISBN 1-56280-113-9 16.95

FOR LOVE AND FOR LIFE: INTIMATE PORTRAITS OF LESBIAN COUPLES by Susan Johnson. 224 pp. ISBN 1-56280-091-4 14.95

DEVOTION by Mindy Kaplan. 192 pp. See the movie — read the book! ISBN 1-56280-093-0 10.95

SOMEONE TO WATCH by Jaye Maiman. 272 pp. A Robin Miller mystery. 4th in a series. ISBN 1-56280-095-7 10.95

GREENER THAN GRASS by Jennifer Fulton. 208 pp. A young woman — a stranger in her bed. ISBN 1-56280-092-2 10.95

TRAVELS WITH DIANA HUNTER by Regine Sands. Erotic lesbian romp. Audio Book (2 cassettes) ISBN 1-56280-107-4 16.95

CABIN FEVER by Carol Schmidt. 256 pp. Sizzling suspense and passion. ISBN 1-56280-089-1 10.95

THERE WILL BE NO GOODBYES by Laura DeHart Young. 192 pp. Romantic love, strength, and friendship. ISBN 1-56280-103-1 10.95

FAULTLINE by Sheila Ortiz Taylor. 144 pp. Joyous comic
lesbian novel.   ISBN 1-56280-108-2   9.95

OPEN HOUSE by Pat Welch. 176 pp. P.I. Helen Black's fourth
case.   ISBN 1-56280-102-3   10.95

ONCE MORE WITH FEELING by Peggy J. Herring. 240 pp.
Lighthearted, loving romantic adventure.   ISBN 1-56280-089-2   10.95

FOREVER by Evelyn Kennedy. 224 pp. Passionate romance — love
overcoming all obstacles.   ISBN 1-56280-094-9   10.95

WHISPERS by Kris Bruyer. 176 pp. Romantic ghost story
                                         ISBN 1-56280-082-5   10.95

NIGHT SONGS by Penny Mickelbury. 224 pp. A Gianna
Maglione Mystery. Second in a series.   ISBN 1-56280-097-3   10.95

GETTING TO THE POINT by Teresa Stores. 256 pp. Classic
southern Lesbian novel.   ISBN 1-56280-100-7   10.95

PAINTED MOON by Karin Kallmaker. 224 pp. Delicious
Kallmaker romance.   ISBN 1-56280-075-2   10.95

THE MYSTERIOUS NAIAD edited by Katherine V. Forrest &
Barbara Grier. 320 pp. Love stories by Naiad Press authors.
                                         ISBN 1-56280-074-4   14.95

DAUGHTERS OF A CORAL DAWN by Katherine V. Forrest.
240 pp. Tenth Anniversay Edition.   ISBN 1-56280-104-X   10.95

BODY GUARD by Claire McNab. 208 pp. A Carol Ashton Mystery.
6th in a series.   ISBN 1-56280-073-6   10.95

CACTUS LOVE by Lee Lynch. 192 pp. Stories by the beloved
storyteller.   ISBN 1-56280-071-X   9.95

SECOND GUESS by Rose Beecham. 216 pp. An Amanda Valentine
Mystery. 2nd in a series.   ISBN 1-56280-069-8   9.95

THE SURE THING by Melissa Hartman. 208 pp. L.A. earthquake
romance.   ISBN 1-56280-078-7   9.95

A RAGE OF MAIDENS by Lauren Wright Douglas. 240 pp. A
Caitlin Reece Mystery. 6th in a series.   ISBN 1-56280-068-X   10.95

TRIPLE EXPOSURE by Jackie Calhoun. 224 pp. Romantic drama
involving many characters.   ISBN 1-56280-067-1   9.95

UP, UP AND AWAY by Catherine Ennis. 192 pp. Delightful
romance.   ISBN 1-56280-065-5   9.95

PERSONAL ADS by Robbi Sommers. 176 pp. Sizzling short
stories.   ISBN 1-56280-059-0   9.95

FLASHPOINT by Katherine V. Forrest. 256 pp. Lesbian
blockbuster!   ISBN 1-56280-043-4   22.95

CROSSWORDS by Penny Sumner. 256 pp. 2nd Victoria Cross
Mystery.   ISBN 1-56280-064-7   9.95

SWEET CHERRY WINE by Carol Schmidt. 224 pp. A novel of
suspense.   ISBN 1-56280-063-9   9.95
CERTAIN SMILES by Dorothy Tell. 160 pp. Erotic short stories.
                                             ISBN 1-56280-066-3   9.95
EDITED OUT by Lisa Haddock. 224 pp. 1st Carmen Ramirez
Mystery.   ISBN 1-56280-077-9   9.95
WEDNESDAY NIGHTS by Camarin Grae. 288 pp. Sexy
adventure.   ISBN 1-56280-060-4   10.95
SMOKEY O by Celia Cohen. 176 pp. Relationships on the
playing field.   ISBN 1-56280-057-4   9.95
KATHLEEN O'DONALD by Penny Hayes. 256 pp. Rose and
Kathleen find each other and employment in 1909 NYC.
                                             ISBN 1-56280-070-1   9.95
STAYING HOME by Elisabeth Nonas. 256 pp. Molly and Alix
want a baby . . . or do they?   ISBN 1-56280-076-0   10.95
TRUE LOVE by Jennifer Fulton. 240 pp. Six lesbians searching
for love in all the "right" places.   ISBN 1-56280-035-3   10.95
GARDENIAS WHERE THERE ARE NONE by Molleen Zanger.
176 pp. Why is Melanie inextricably drawn to the old house?
                                             ISBN 1-56280-056-6   9.95
KEEPING SECRETS by Penny Mickelbury. 208 pp. A Gianna
Maglione Mystery. First in a series.   ISBN 1-56280-052-3   9.95
THE ROMANTIC NAIAD edited by Katherine V. Forrest &
Barbara Grier. 336 pp. Love stories by Naiad Press authors.
                                             ISBN 1-56280-054-X   14.95
UNDER MY SKIN by Jaye Maiman. 336 pp. A Robin Miller
mystery. 3rd in a series.   ISBN 1-56280-049-3.   10.95
STAY TOONED by Rhonda Dicksion. 144 pp. Cartoons — 1st
collection since *Lesbian Survival Manual.*   ISBN 1-56280-045-0   9.95
CAR POOL by Karin Kallmaker. 272pp. Lesbians on wheels
and then some!   ISBN 1-56280-048-5   10.95
NOT TELLING MOTHER: STORIES FROM A LIFE by Diane
Salvatore. 176 pp. Her 3rd novel.   ISBN 1-56280-044-2   9.95
GOBLIN MARKET by Lauren Wright Douglas. 240pp. A Caitlin
Reece Mystery. 5th in a series.   ISBN 1-56280-047-7   10.95
LONG GOODBYES by Nikki Baker. 256 pp. A Virginia Kelly
mystery. 3rd in a series.   ISBN 1-56280-042-6   9.95
FRIENDS AND LOVERS by Jackie Calhoun. 224 pp. Mid-western
Lesbian lives and loves.   ISBN 1-56280-041-8   10.95
THE CAT CAME BACK by Hilary Mullins. 208 pp. Highly
praised Lesbian novel.   ISBN 1-56280-040-X   9.95

BEHIND CLOSED DOORS by Robbi Sommers. 192 pp. Hot,
erotic short stories.   ISBN 1-56280-039-6   9.95

CLAIRE OF THE MOON by Nicole Conn. 192 pp. See the
movie — read the book!   ISBN 1-56280-038-8   10.95

SILENT HEART by Claire McNab. 192 pp. Exotic Lesbian
romance.   ISBN 1-56280-036-1   10.95

HAPPY ENDINGS by Kate Brandt. 272 pp. Intimate conversations
with Lesbian authors.   ISBN 1-56280-050-7   10.95

THE SPY IN QUESTION by Amanda Kyle Williams. 256 pp.
4th Madison McGuire.   ISBN 1-56280-037-X   9.95

SAVING GRACE by Jennifer Fulton. 240 pp. Adventure and
romantic entanglement.   ISBN 1-56280-051-5   9.95

THE YEAR SEVEN by Molleen Zanger. 208 pp. Women surviving
in a new world.   ISBN 1-56280-034-5   9.95

CURIOUS WINE by Katherine V. Forrest. 176 pp. Tenth Anniver-
sary Edition. The most popular contemporary Lesbian love story.
                                         ISBN 1-56280-053-1   10.95
     Audio Book (2 cassettes)   ISBN 1-56280-105-8   16.95

CHAUTAUQUA by Catherine Ennis. 192 pp. Exciting, romantic
adventure.   ISBN 1-56280-032-9   9.95

A PROPER BURIAL by Pat Welch. 192 pp. A Helen Black
mystery. 3rd in a series.   ISBN 1-56280-033-7   9.95

SILVERLAKE HEAT: A Novel of Suspense by Carol Schmidt.
240 pp. Rhonda is as hot as Laney's dreams.   ISBN 1-56280-031-0   9.95

LOVE, ZENA BETH by Diane Salvatore. 224 pp. The most talked
about lesbian novel of the nineties!   ISBN 1-56280-030-2   10.95

A DOORYARD FULL OF FLOWERS by Isabel Miller. 160 pp.
Stories incl. 2 sequels to *Patience and Sarah.*   ISBN 1-56280-029-9   9.95

MURDER BY TRADITION by Katherine V. Forrest. 288 pp. A
Kate Delafield Mystery. 4th in a series.   ISBN 1-56280-002-7   10.95

THE EROTIC NAIAD edited by Katherine V. Forrest & Barbara
Grier. 224 pp. Love stories by Naiad Press authors.
                                         ISBN 1-56280-026-4   13.95

DEAD CERTAIN by Claire McNab. 224 pp. A Carol Ashton
mystery. 5th in a series.   ISBN 1-56280-027-2   9.95

CRAZY FOR LOVING by Jaye Maiman. 320 pp. A Robin Miller
mystery. 2nd in a series.   ISBN 1-56280-025-6   9.95

These are just a few of the many Naiad Press titles — we are the oldest and
largest lesbian/feminist publishing company in the world. Please request a
complete catalog. We offer personal service; we encourage and welcome
direct mail orders from individuals who have limited access to bookstores
carrying our publications.